WHAT DO REAL PIGEONS DO?

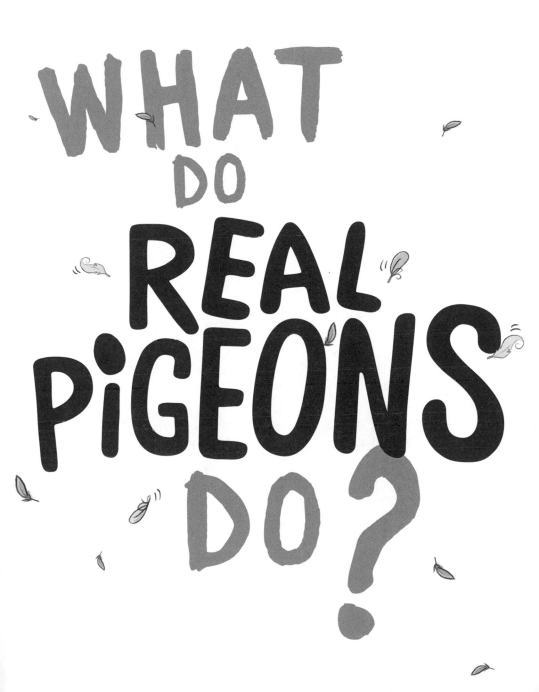

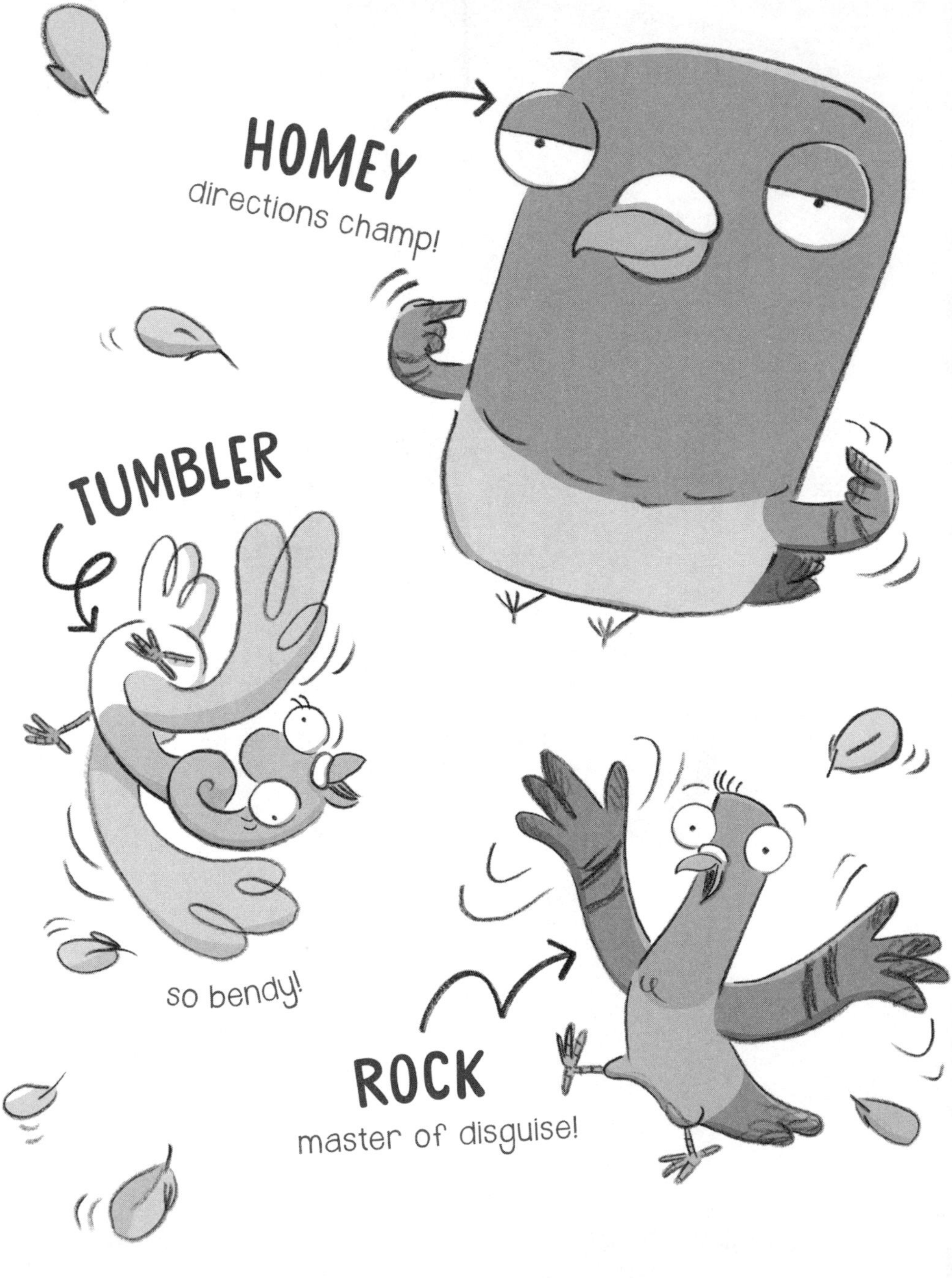
HOMEY
directions champ!
TUMBLER
so bendy!
ROCK
master of disguise!

REAL PIGEONS

1

FIGHT CRIME!

FRILLBACK
superstrong!

RANDOM HOUSE 🏠 NEW YORK

ANDREW McDONALD and BEN WOOD

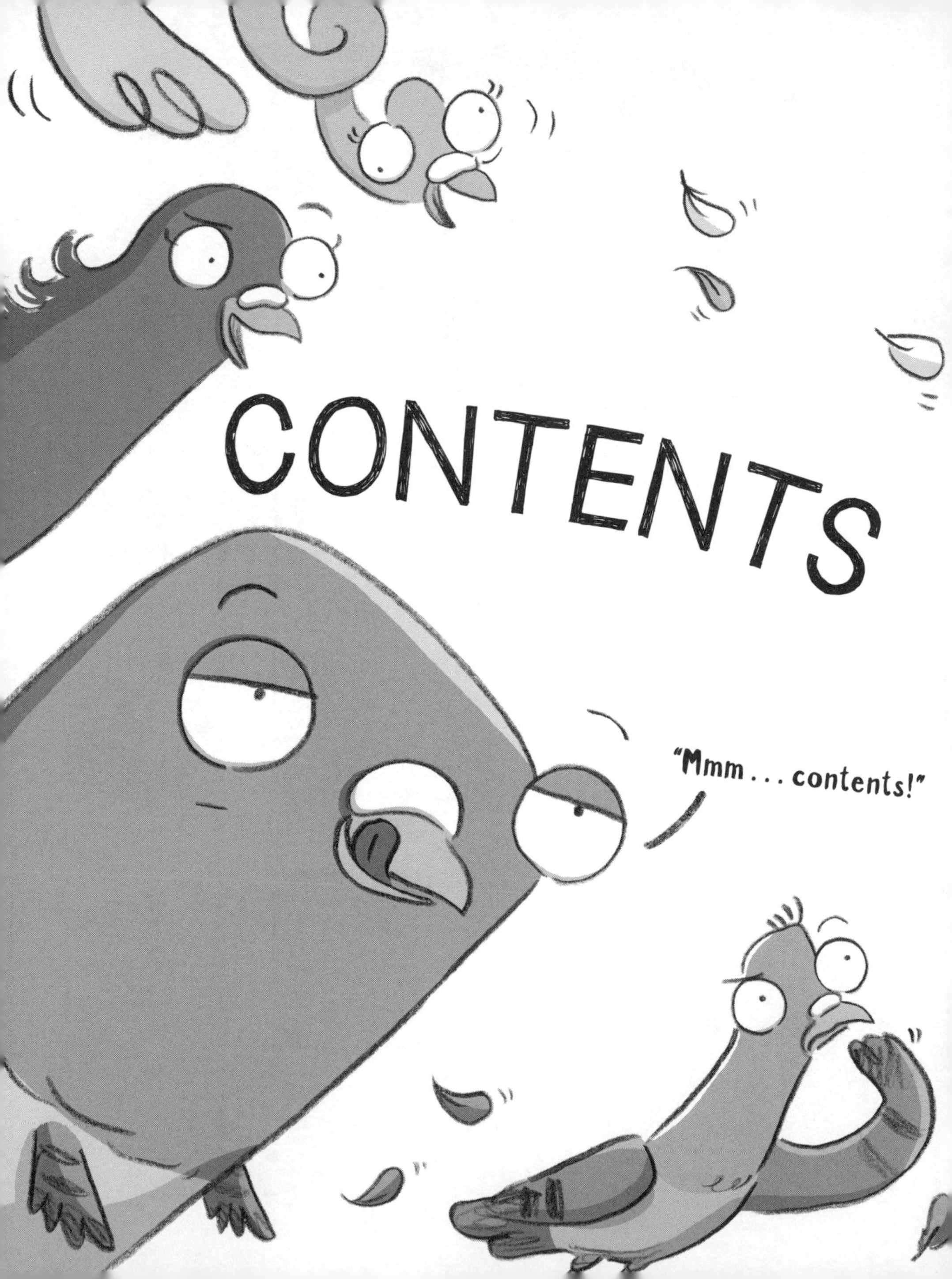
CONTENTS
"Mmm . . . contents!"

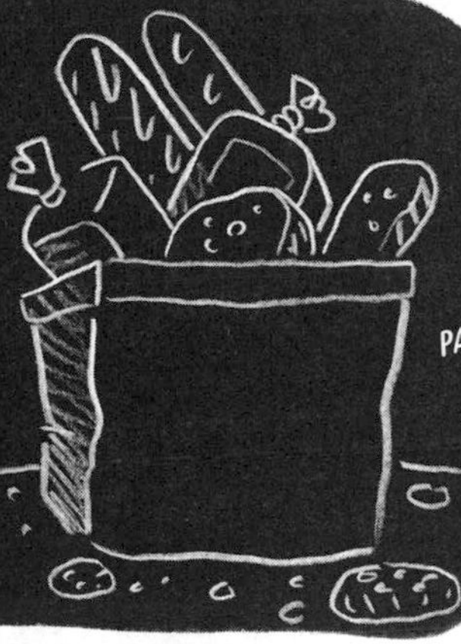

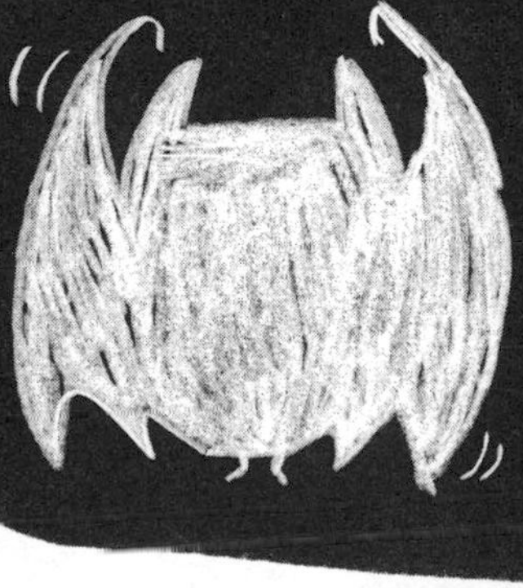

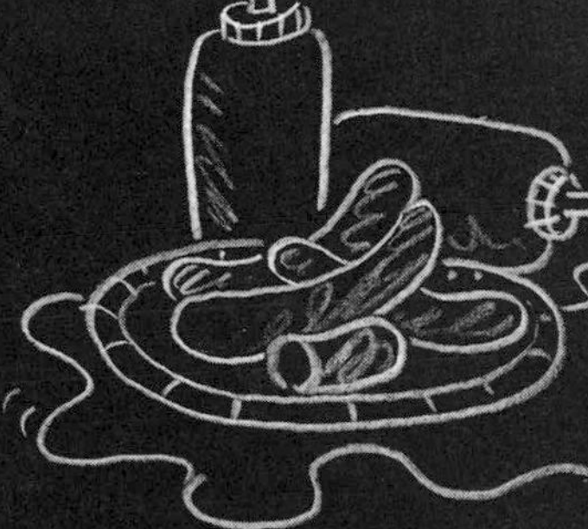

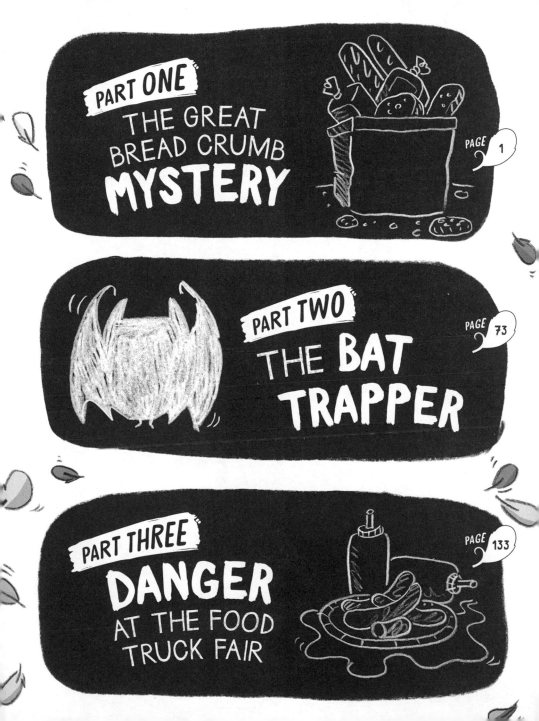

FOR PETER MCDONALD —ANDREW

FOR DAVE CARTER —BEN

Text copyright © 2018 by Andrew McDonald
Cover art and interior illustrations copyright © 2018 by Ben Wood
Series design copyright © 2018 Hardie Grant Egmont

Visit us on the Web! rhcbooks.com

Educators and librarians, for a variety of teaching tools, visit us at
RHTeachersLibrarians.com

Library of Congress Cataloging-in-Publication Data is available on request.
ISBN 978-0-593-11942-6 (hc) | ISBN 978-0-593-11943-3 (lib. bdg.) |
ISBN 978-0-593-11944-0 (ebook)

Printed in the United States of America
10 9 8 7 6 5 4 3
First American Edition

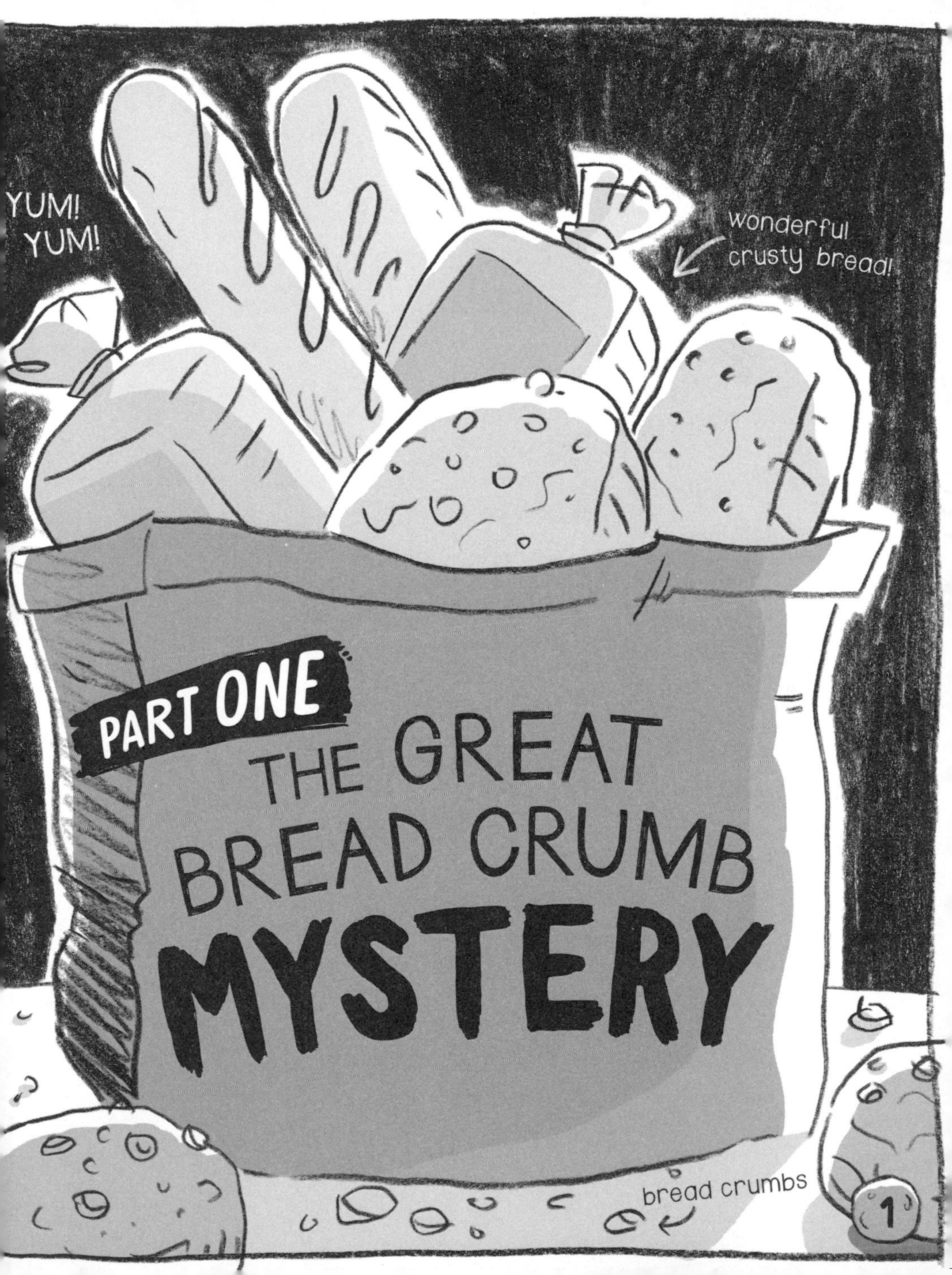
YUM! YUM!
wonderful crusty bread!
PART ONE
THE GREAT BREAD CRUMB MYSTERY
bread crumbs
1

CHAPTER 1

Which one of these is a pigeon?

PIGEON?

"Munch!"

"Munch!"

"Munch!"

PIGEON?

PIGEON?

"Am I?"

If you thought it
was the **rooster**—

CORRECT!

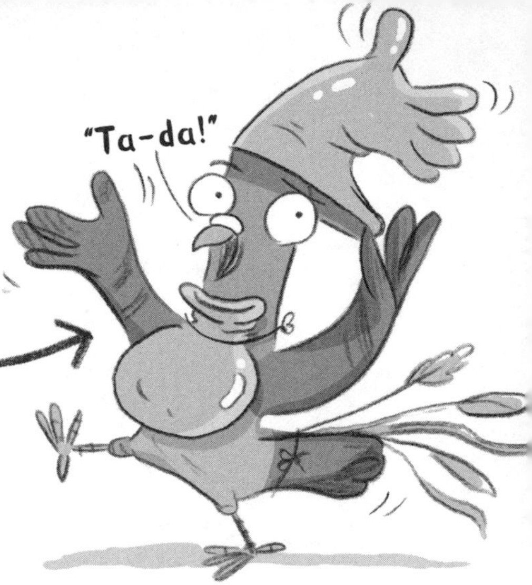
"Ta-da!"

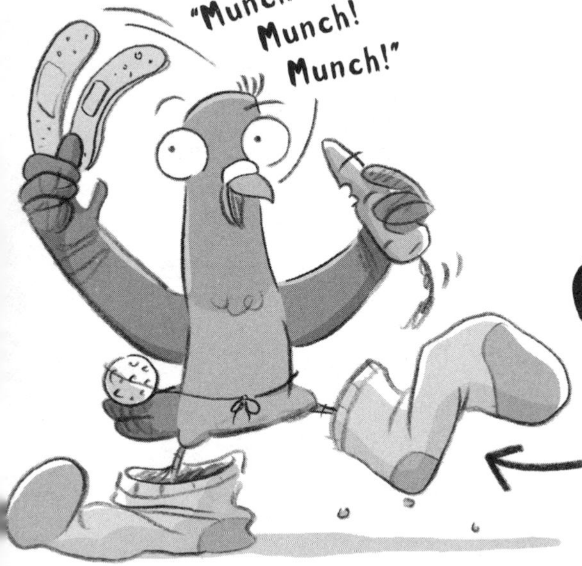
"Munch!
Munch!
Munch!"

If you thought it
was the **rabbit**—

CORRECT!

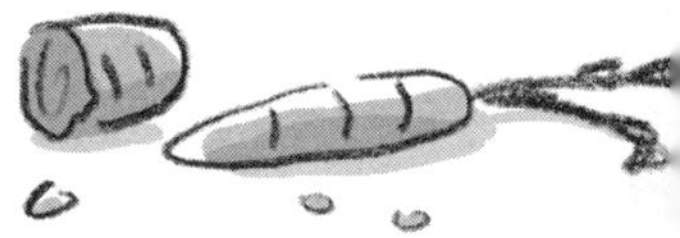

If you thought it was
the **caterpillar**—

NO.

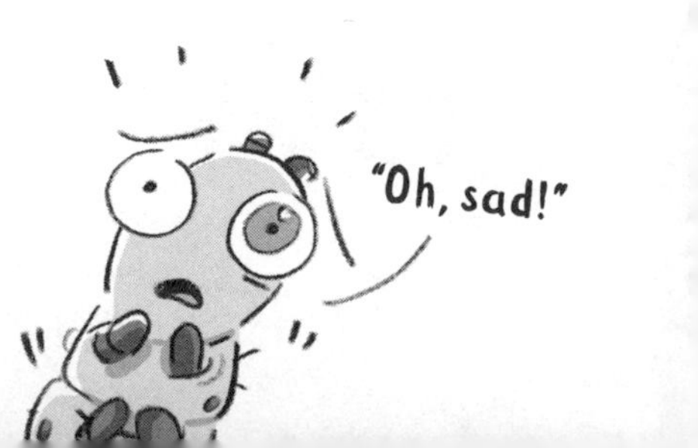
"Oh, sad!"

But it **WAS** the pile of leaves!

"Oh, happy!"

This is Rock Pigeon. He is a big fan of nature.

He enjoys dressing up like his favorite plants and animals.

"We're an inspiration!"

But Rock is still a pigeon.

And like all pigeons, he **LOVES** bread crumbs.

"Yum! Yum! Yum!"

Bread crumbs are the most delicious food in the world for a pigeon.

Do you like french fries? Pizza? Chocolate ice cream? That is what bread crumbs taste like to pigeons.

ABSOLUTE HEAVEN!

Rock lives on a farm with a flock of pigeons,

some farm animals,

and a pack of llamas.

None of the farm animals understand why Rock dresses up.

The cows think he is silly.

"REAL PIGEONS DON'T WEAR COSTUMES!"

The pigeons think he should just be a pigeon.

"REAL PIGEONS SHOULD DO PIGEON THINGS!"

And the llamas think he's a show-off.

But llamas are just like that. They think everyone is a show-off.

Rock doesn't care, though. He does whatever he wants!

One day, an old pigeon
shows up at the farm.

"I'm looking for someone who
likes dressing up," says the old
pigeon. "I've heard birds tweeting
about him in these parts."

"THAT'S ME!" says a rose.

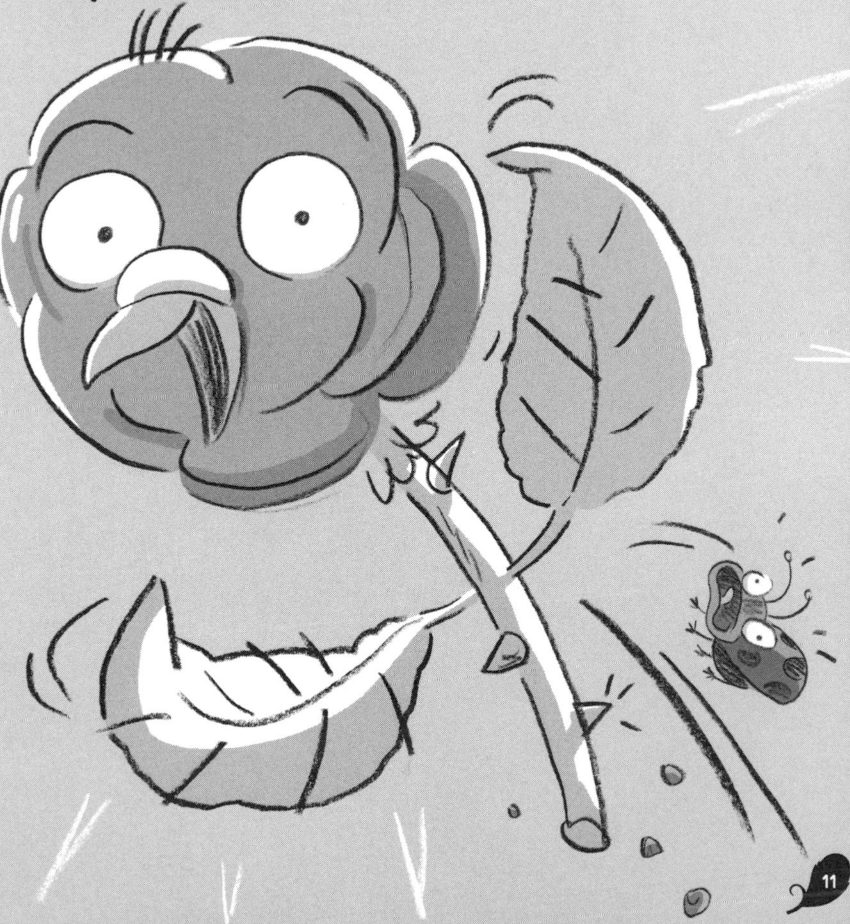

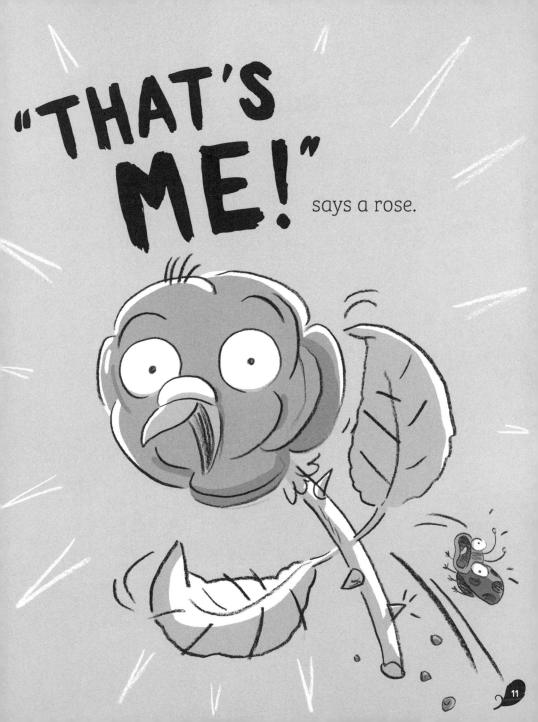

"My name is Grandpouter Pigeon,"

says the old pigeon.

"I'm starting a squad of crime-fighting pigeons. We need a MASTER OF DISGUISE. Want to come to the city and join us?"

Rock isn't sure.

"Dressing up to fight crime sounds exciting," he says. "But I like living on the farm!"

"MOO."

"Why don't you come and help with a case?" asks Grandpouter. "Then make a decision. We need a pigeon like you."

"**OK—why not?**" says Rock.

And they take off.

"Those pigeons are flying away!"

"**SHOW-OFFS!**"

Rock and Grandpouter fly over mountains and glide through valleys.

"Why are you recruiting *pigeons*?" asks Rock.

"Pigeons are **PERFECT** for fighting crime," explains Grandpouter.

farm

pointy mountain

valleys

city

"Show-offs!"

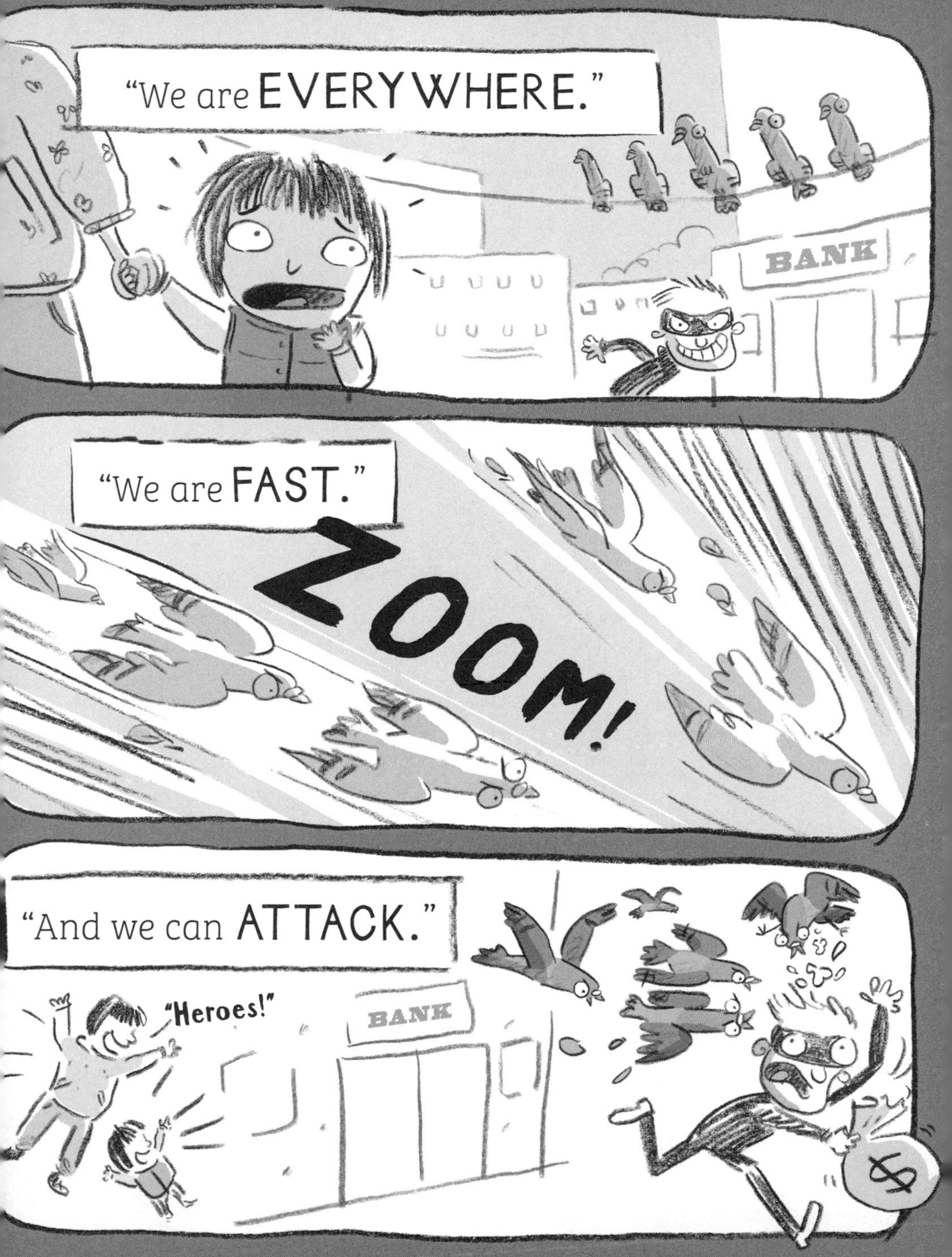
"We are EVERYWHERE."
BANK
"We are FAST."
ZOOM!
"And we can ATTACK."
"Heroes!"
BANK

"Plus, all the pigeons I've picked for the squad have special **PIGEON POWERS!**" says Grandpouter.

But Rock is worried about the crime-fighting. What if they come across **SCARY** things?

Like birdcatchers?

robber

birdcage

innocent bird

Or crows?

beady eyes

scary pointy feathers

beak, sharp like scissors—probably for snipping enemies

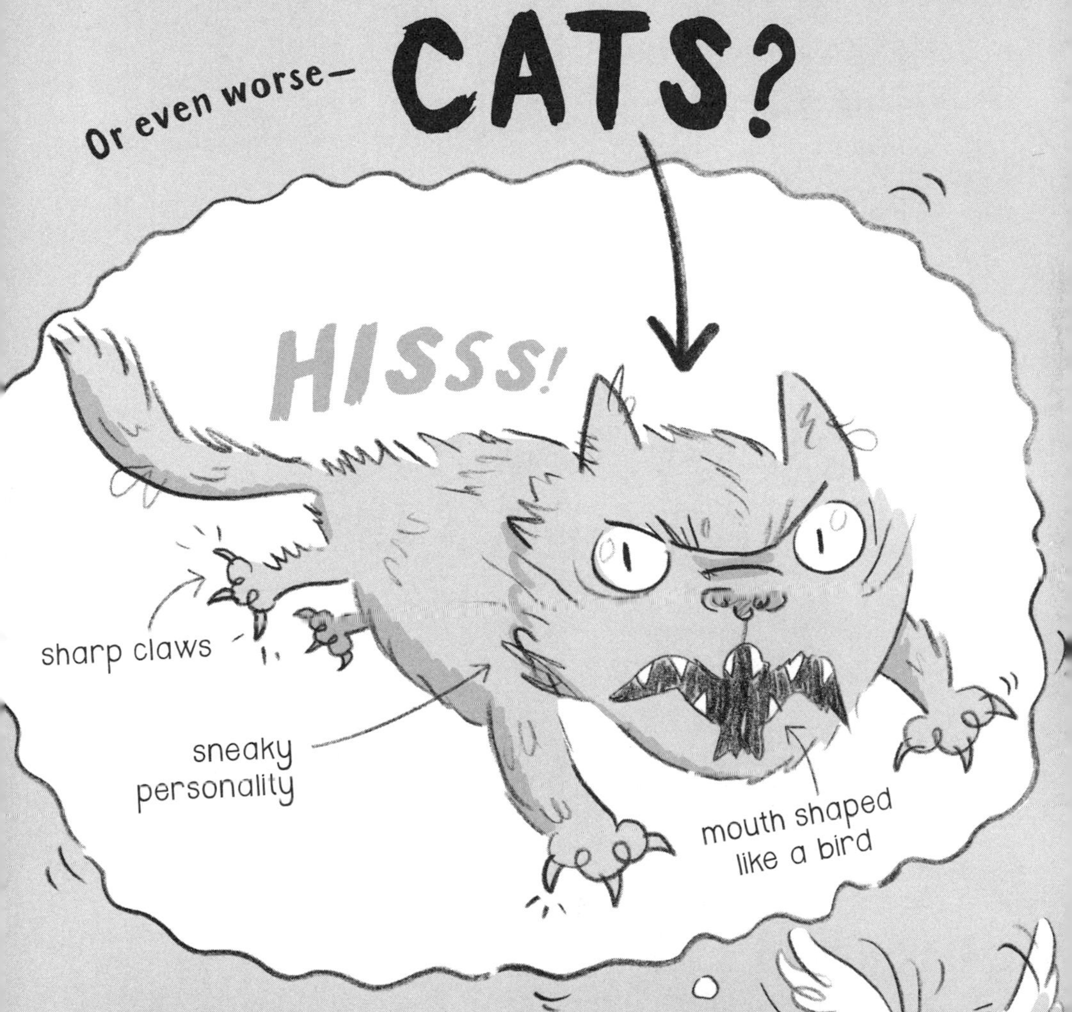
Or even worse—
CATS?
HISSS!
sharp claws
sneaky personality
mouth shaped like a bird

Rock has never really thought about it before, but . . . sometimes animals can be scary!

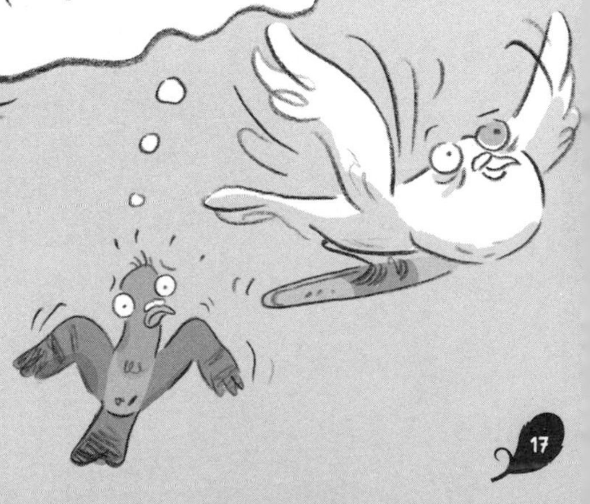

He forgets all that when they arrive in the city, though, because there are parks everywhere.

PARKS FULL OF BREAD CRUMBS!

bread crumbs!

more bread crumbs!!

even more bread crumbs!

18

How would you feel about a park full of pizza, french fries, and ice cream?

That's how Rock feels now.
VERY HAPPY!

"YUM!"

so many!

here too!

even here!

Rock and Grandpouter land in one of the parks.

"This is where I live," says Grandpouter. "Take a look around—there's something weird going on in this park."

"Hmmm."

"Hmmm."

"Hmmm."

"Hmmm."

Everything seems normal to Rock. Then it hits him. "Where are the bread crumbs?"

"Exactly," says Grandpouter.
"All the bread crumbs in this park
have mysteriously vanished."

NOOOOOOOOOOOOOO!"

CHAPTER 2

Rock can't believe it.

There were **ALWAYS** bread crumbs at the farm.

"Hello, pigeons!"

So how can an entire park have no bread crumbs?

At that moment, some new pigeons swoop down.

"Ah, they're here," says Grandpouter. "Rock, meet the rest of the squad."

FRILLBACK PIGEON

TUMBLER PIGEON

HOMING PIGEON
(nickname: Homey)

"Found you, dudes!"

23

Grandpouter leans forward on his walking stick. "Welcome, pigeons," he says. "The mystery of the missing bread crumbs is our first case. Have you found any clues?"

"I found something." Frillback holds up a bread crumb.

"I didn't think there were any crumbs left in this park!" says Rock.

"This is the only one!"

says Homey.

"I found it by the water fountain," says Frillback. "We must look after it and— HEY!"

BREAD-UURRPPPP!"

Homey has eaten the bread crumb.

"Homey, that was our only clue!" cries Tumbler.

"And you ATE it!" adds Frillback.

"Sorry, PIGS," says Homey with a shrug. "I couldn't help myself."

"We should be solving the mystery.
Not making up names."

Their first case is off to a rocky start.

"All of you—go stake out the water fountain," says Grandpouter. "See if any more bread crumbs show up. Use your PIGEON POWERS to make sure no one sees you."

Rock smiles.

IT'S TIME TO BE A
MASTER OF DISGUISE.

The stakeout begins.

Each pigeon gets into position.

Frillback hides in some acorns.

Homey hides up high in a tree.

"I always know how to find the BIRD'S-EYE VIEW!"

Tumbler hides in
the water fountain.

And—of course—Rock hides with a disguise.

The pigeons wait and watch.

But nothing happens.

The park is quiet.

Hours go by.

Until there is a sudden
flash of color.

IT'S A CAT!

CRINKLE
CRINKLE

KWISPIES

Rock shivers.
His costume crinkles loudly.

Thankfully, the cat doesn't notice.

It keeps running and is soon gone.
The cat is the first creature to go past all day!

The pigeons haven't seen any other animals.
Or humans.

Suddenly, Rock remembers something.

"Hello, pigeons!"

farmer
(human)

Bread crumbs come from humans!

"There are no bread crumbs in this park," he cries, "because there are no **HUMANS** in this park!"

Rock has solved the mystery of the missing bread crumbs.

But now there is a bigger mystery.

"Where are all the HUMANS?"

"Where can we look for humans?" asks Rock.

"I know a place," says Homey. "This way, PIGS!"

"I'll keep watch!"

Homey takes them to a tree at the edge of the park.

Across the street they see a man.

happy customer

BAKERY

"So humans still exist," says Rock.

"True," says Frillback.
"They just aren't in the park."

While the others are talking, Homey flies off to the bakery.

"I can smell bread crumbs," he says.

"I MUST HAVE THEM!"

But the baker is not welcoming.

"We have to help him," says Rock as the baker chases Homey around the shop.

"I guess so," Frillback groans. "But how?"

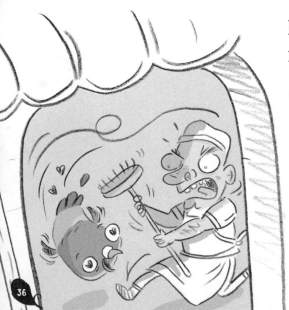

Luckily, Rock has a plan.

The pigeons make their move.

so frilly!

A lady with a very **FRILLY** hat walks into the bakery.

Little does she know she's now carrying two clever birds.

The lady tries to buy some bread.

But Homey is still causing mayhem.

"Birds fly in here sometimes," explains the girl at the counter. "Probably to escape the park across the street. People say it's haunted."

Is the park really haunted? Rock hasn't seen any ghosts.

Suddenly, a cat leaps onto the counter.
The same cat from the park!

HISSS!

The cat snarls. **"REAL PIGEONS
STAY AWAY FROM CATS!"**

Rock shakes with fear.

"I don't think
your cat
likes me!"

"It's not my cat.
It just comes in
here sometimes."

Rock and Frillback grab Homey.
They fly out of the bakery.

"Time to go!"

"I just wanted to eat a bread crumb," moans Homey.

CHAPTER 3

All the pigeons meet on top of the gazebo again.

Grandpouter is worried. He has been meeting animals in the city. Animals who used to live in his park.

"Something scared them away," says Grandpouter. "But what?"

"The humans are scared too," says Frillback. "They think the park is haunted. That cat is the only one who isn't scared!"

"Then we need to find that cat!" says Homey. "Follow me, PIGS!"

"I still don't like that nickname."

But Rock stops. He doesn't want to see that cat again.

"Come on, Rock — the early bird catches the cat!"

Rock thinks about flying back to the farm.
And forgetting about crime-fighting.

Until he remembers all the animals who got
scared out of the park.

"No one should be scaring animals away! **EVER!**"

So he takes a deep breath.
And follows the others.

But they don't find the cat.

They find something much, **MUCH** scarier.

A MONSTER CROW!

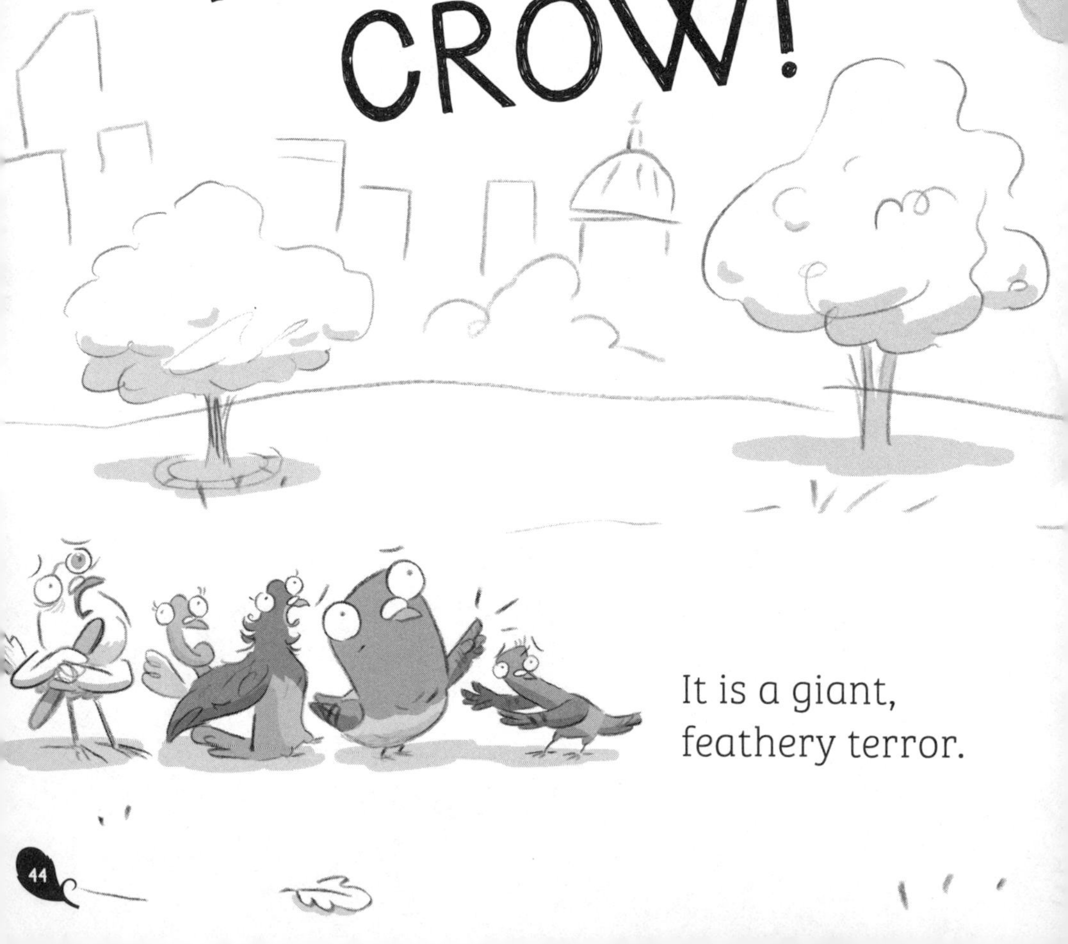

It is a giant, feathery terror.

"CAWWWW!"

No wonder the park is empty.

Frillback bravely tries to fight the **MONSTER CROW.**

But she doesn't get very far.

"STAY AWAY! We hate pigeons!"

Rock is scared stiff. But the park is for everyone. Not just **MONSTER CROWS.**

And he's just had an idea.

"I can get close to the **MONSTER CROW,**" he says, "if I dress up as a crow."

It's time for Rock to use his **PIGEON POWER.**

He covers his legs in mud.

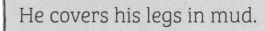

He asks for some sharp feathers from a magpie.

He finds half of a chocolate bar and makes it into a pointy beak.

And he practices having beady eyes.

Now Rock Pigeon is **ROCK CROW.**

The other pigeons hide.

And Rock marches forward, trying to act like a crow.

"Hello," Rock says.
"I am also a crow.
I hate pigeons too.
They look like doves
made out of cobwebs."

"Hello, little crow!"
bellows the MONSTER CROW.

When it speaks, its
voice echoes deeply
through the park.

But as Rock gets closer, he sees the truth about the **MONSTER CROW.**

It is actually a bunch of crows flying together in the shape of a big crow.

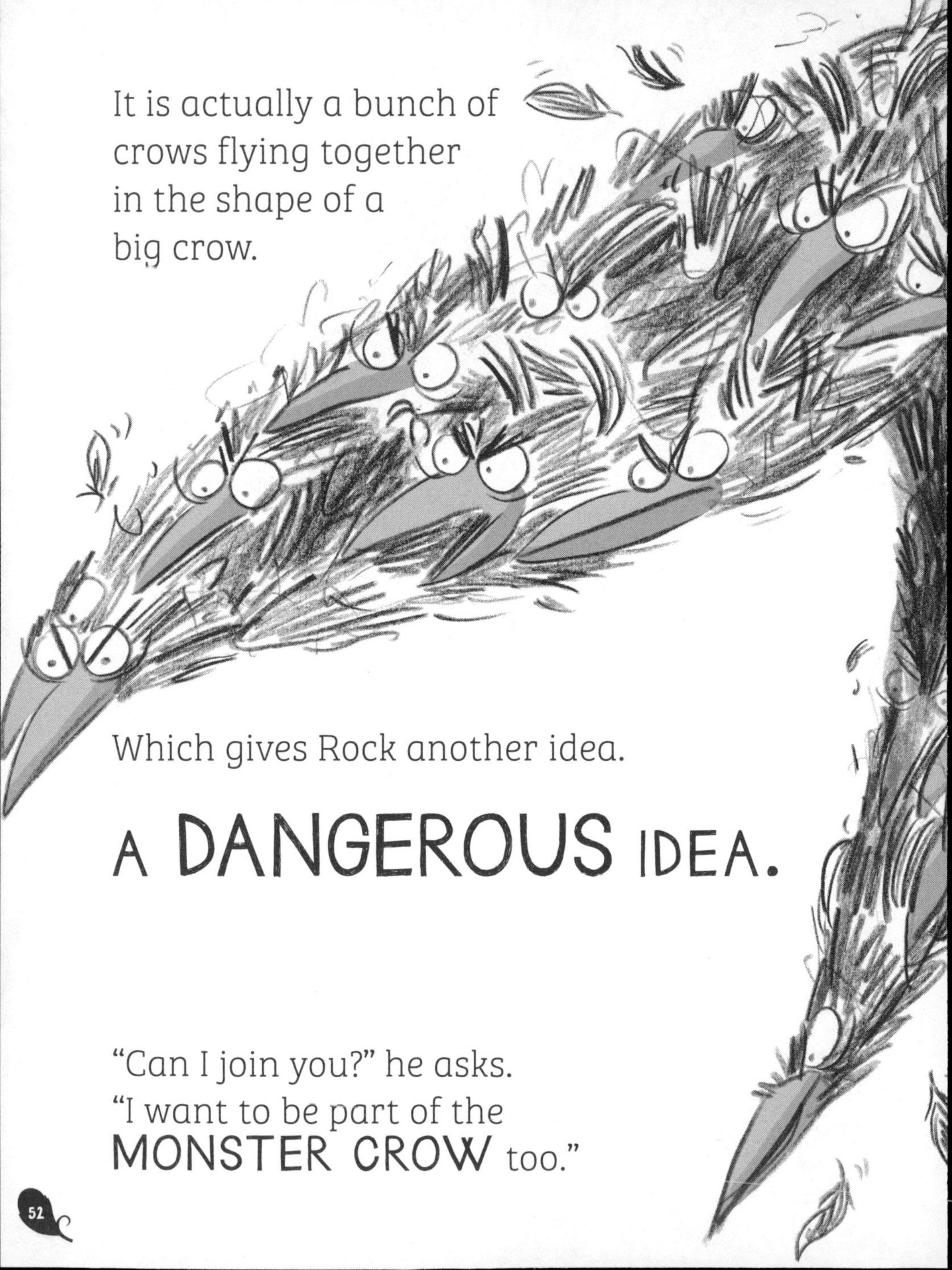

Which gives Rock another idea.

A DANGEROUS IDEA.

"Can I join you?" he asks. "I want to be part of the MONSTER CROW too."

"Yes," say all the crows. "Fly up and be part of our throat."

"Thanks," says Rock. "Why are we pretending to be a **MONSTER CROW** anyway?"

"Because we are sick of sharing the park," the crows say. "There are too many pigeons. And too many humans. So we are scaring everyone away. Our boss showed us how to do it. We want a park just for crows."

"Your boss?" asks Rock. "Who is that?"

But something is wrong.

DRIP!

DRIP!

DRIP!

"Your beak is MELTING!"
the crows cry.

Rock looks down.

Chocolate is dripping
to the ground. This is bad.

The crows are angry.

"You're not a crow!" they scream.

They clean Rock's legs.

They pluck his magpie feathers.

And they get rid of his chocolate beak.

"**What do we have here?**"

says a voice.

"Hello, boss," say the crows.

Rock turns around. He freezes with shock.

It is the cat.

"Do you like my MONSTER CROW?" says the cat. "It's helping to turn this into a CROW PARK."

"Why do you care about crows?" asks Rock. "You're a cat."

The cat gives an evil grin and says,

"Am I?"

CHAPTER 4

The cat takes off its head.

"You're not the only one who can play **DRESS-UP!**"

"I am Jungle Crow," says the bird. "King of the crows!"

Jungle Crow is scarier than any cat.

Rock takes a step back. "Why were you pretending to be a cat?"

"Those bakers chase birds away," says Jungle Crow. "But not cats. It was easy to steal bread to feed my crows."

So *that's* where Frillback's single bread crumb came from.

"But stealing is a c-c-crime!" stammers Rock.

"I don't care,"
snarls Jungle Crow.

"Now **GET OUT OF HERE!**
This is a **CROW PARK!**
**REAL PIGEONS DON'T ARGUE
WITH CROWS!"**

"I don't think so," says a familiar voice. It's Frillback.

And Grandpouter. And Tumbler. And Homey!

Rock is overjoyed.

"Actually . . . ," he says.

"REAL PIGEONS FIGHT CRIME!"

"Nice work, Rock!" says Grandpouter. "Now let's finish this. Frillback, use your **PIGEON POWER!**"

"Roger that!" Frillback strides over and kicks the tree trunk.

Acorns slam down from the tree—
making the crows panic and fly off!

The **MONSTER CROW** is no more.

"NOOOOOO!"
cries Jungle Crow.

"You're finished, Jungle Crow," says Grandpouter.

"Pesky pigeons," grumbles Jungle Crow. He grabs his bag of bread and flies off.

Rock wishes he had taken one of those loaves. Then he sees Homey.

"We deserve a victory snack," says Homey. **"So I snagged one."**

The pigeons return to the gazebo.

"The mystery is solved!" Grandpouter says.

The pigeons all high-five.

Very quietly.

Feathers don't make much noise.

"Bread crumbs will start showing up again," says Rock, "when the humans return."

"Let's call the other animals back too," says Grandpouter.

"The MONSTER CROW is gone!"

"Pass it on!"

The message is heard far and wide.

Birds and animals return to the park.

"Hooray!"

"Hoot!"

"Yay!"

"Quack!"

Rock realizes that he DOES want to fight crime. Because he won't just be dressing up like animals. He'll be HELPING them.

"I want to join the squad," he says.

Grandpouter smiles. "I'm glad to hear that," he says. "We can make this gazebo our **PIGEON HEADQUARTERS.** Now we just need a name for our squad."

"I liked what Rock said before," says Frillback.

"REAL PIGEONS FIGHT CRIME!"

"That's us!" cries Tumbler. "We are **REAL PIGEONS!**"

"Or—**REAL PIGS?**" says Homey.

"NO!"

"Don't worry," says Rock, putting a wing around Homey. "You stole Jungle Crow's bread. You're a hero!"

Homey gives the bread to Frillback. Who turns it into bread crumbs.

Then the pigeons eat like crazy.

Rock picks up a big bread crumb in his beak.

He is a **REAL PIGEON** now. His new life
of fighting crime and protecting his fellow
creatures has begun.

He gulps down the bread crumb.

And wonders what
creatures they will
help next.

THE END . . . FOR NOW

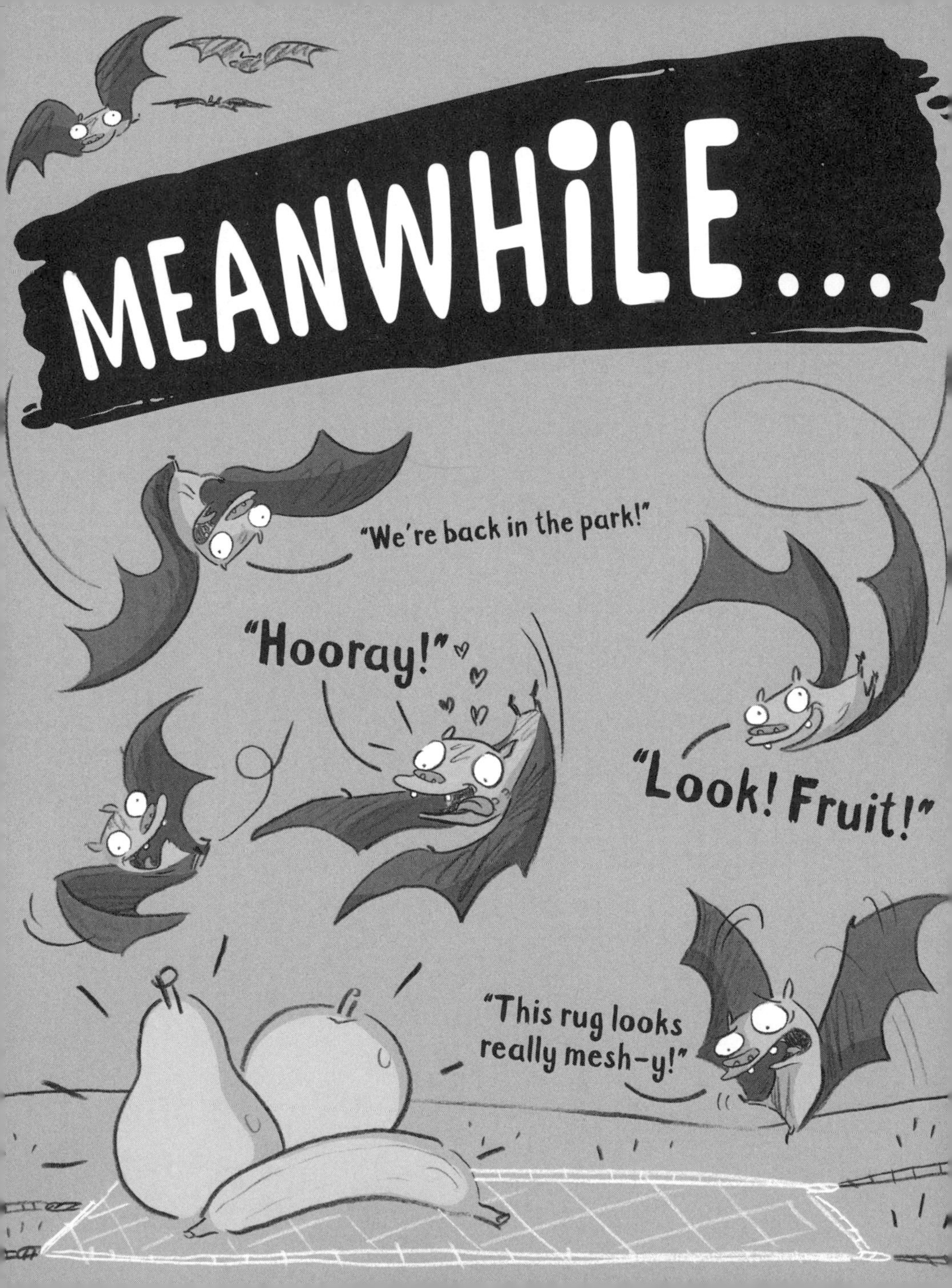
MEANWHILE...
"We're back in the park!"
"Hooray!"
"Look! Fruit!"
"This rug looks really mesh-y!"

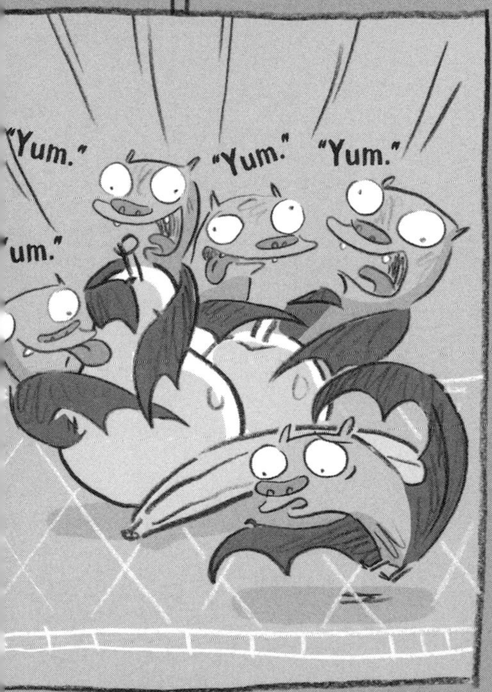
"Yum."
"Yum."
"Yum."
"Yum."
"um."

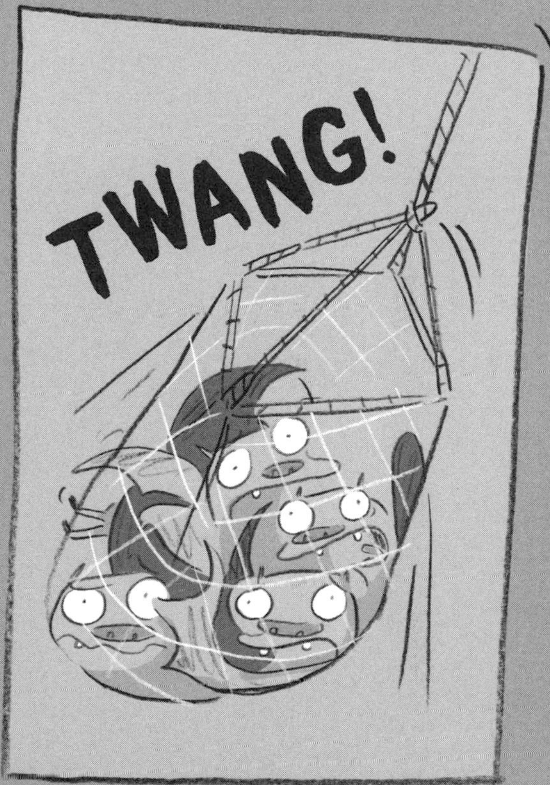
TWANG!

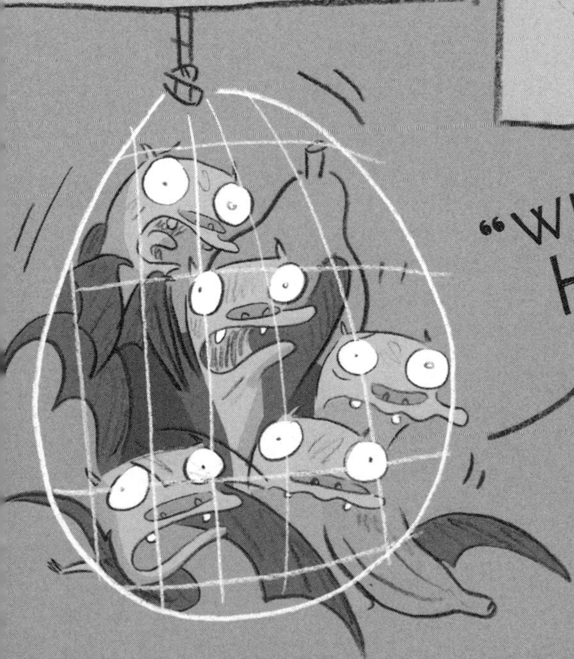

"WHO WILL HELP US NOW?"

cry the bats.

Who do you think?

TO BE CONTINUED . . .

PART TWO
THE BAT TRAPPER

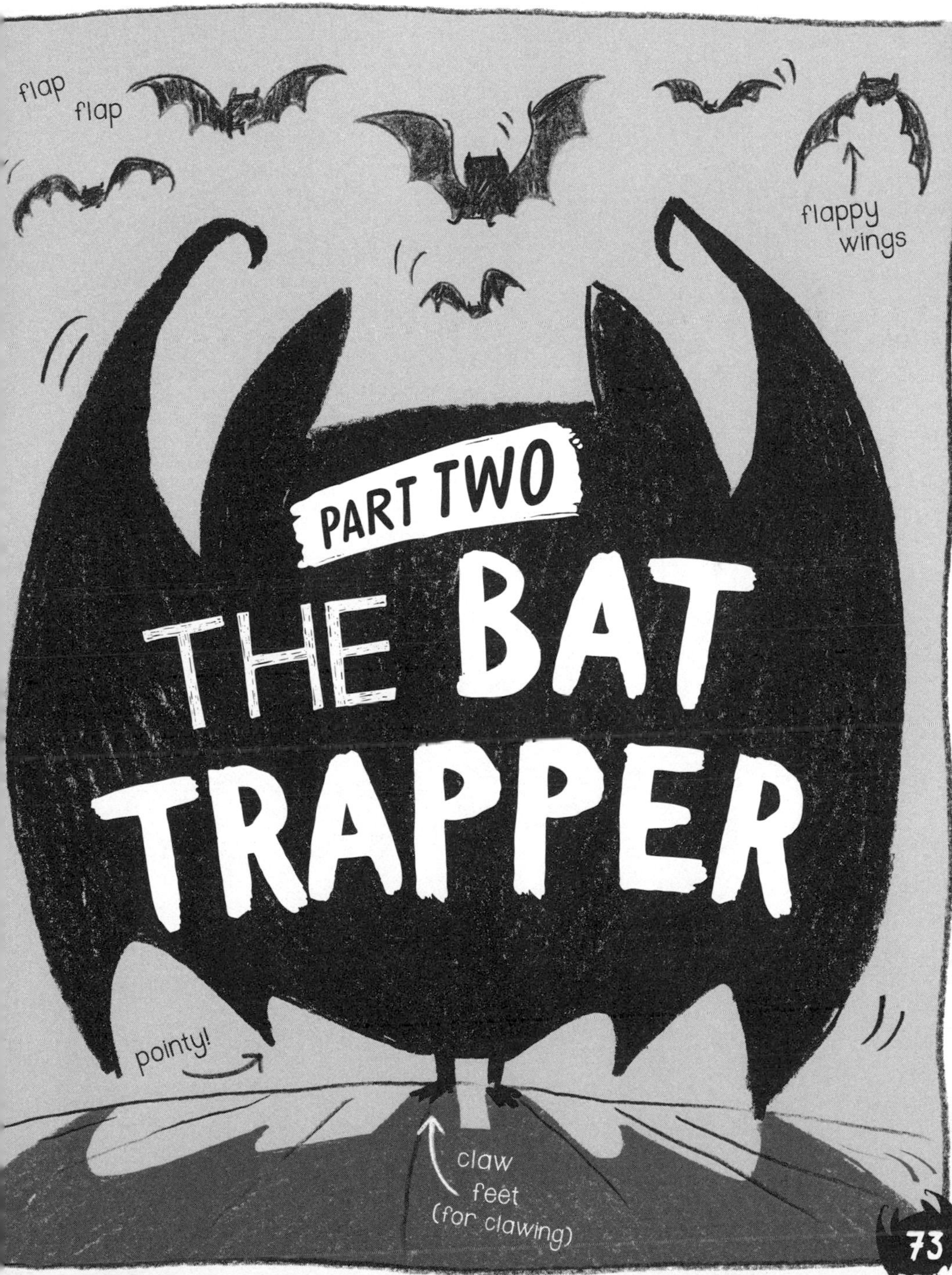
flap
flap
flappy
wings
pointy!
claw
feet
(for clawing)

CHAPTER 1

Rock Pigeon flies
through the air.

He is going somewhere
VERY EXCITING.

A GARBAGE CAN!

But garbuge cans are not exciting.
Are they?

THEY ARE WHEN THEY CONTAIN THE **REAL PIGEONS!**

Garbage cans are great places for secret meetings. No one else ever hangs out in garbage cans.

"I'm in a moldy milkshake."

"I'm on a moldy burger."

"I hate garbage can meetings."

Despite all the garbage can meetings,
Rock loves fighting crime now.

"BEING A REAL PIGEON IS
TOTALLY COO!"

But there is **always**
trouble lurking.

"We have our next mission,"
says Grandpouter.
"The BATS are in trouble!"

**"That's
NOT coo!"**

"Oh no," says Tumbler.
"The bats are my friends!"

Frillback is shocked. "They *are*?"

"Yeah, we fly around at night together sometimes," says Tumbler.

"The bats like it when I use my bendy
PIGEON POWER and do **Flight Moves.**"

THE FLYING STAIRS

THE NEVER-ENDING SERPENT

THE DOUBLE KNOT

"So *that*'s where you've been going at night,"
says Frillback. She is a little jealous.

Rock has never even *seen* a bat before.
"What do they look like?" he asks.

"They have big eyes," says Grandpouter.
"And hairy faces," says Frillback.
"And stretchy wings like leather jackets,"
adds Tumbler.

Rock tries to imagine a bat.

"Come to think of it, I haven't seen the bats
for a few days now," adds Tumbler worriedly.

"That's because they keep getting caught in traps," says Grandpouter. "I've already freed them three nights in a row."

"But one of these days I could be too late," says Grandpouter. "Or maybe they'll get trapped and no one will find them."

"Poor things," says Homey.

"Why would anyone want to trap bats?" asks Rock.

"We have to find this BAT TRAPPER."

"We'll hide on the street tonight to keep watch for the next trap," says Grandpouter. "And rescue the bats again if we have to."

The pigeons all link wings.

"REAL PIGEONS STOP BAT TRAPPERS!"

The **REAL PIGEONS** get ready for a long night.

Rock and Tumbler
fly up to a window ledge.

Tumbler hides in a crack.

Rock rubs green moss
on his body. And puts
twigs in his feathers.

stinky!

twigs

Now he's in **DISGUISE!**

"Hello, Mr. Cactus,"
says Tumbler.

While they wait for the **BAT TRAPPER,** Rock thinks about bats some more. He can't wait to meet them. He loves meeting new animals. Except for crows.

MWAHAHA!

The sun sets.

Black shapes appear in the sky.

The bats are coming.

"Hooray! They haven't been caught in a trap today!"
says Tumbler.

"Are these

BATS?"

asks Rock.

His heart beats faster and faster.
The bats look like . . .

"CROWS!"

he gasps.

CHAPTER 2

The bats get closer.

Rock shrinks into his pot.

On the street, a garbage collector walks past.

"Bats are **CREEPY,**" he says.

"I agree with that guy," says Rock. "I think I might be scared of bats."

"Bats aren't creepy," Tumbler explains. "They're just **nocturnal.** Which means they sleep in the day. And play at night."

She leaps out of her crack with excitement.

The bats see her and swoop down.

"Helloooo! You're not trapped tonight!"

"We love being FREEEEEE!" the bats sing.

The biggest bat does a somersault.

swirly!

Then a twist.

twirly!

Lands on the ledge.

Flips himself over.

And takes a bow.

91

Then he wraps Tumbler in a hug.

"If it isn't my favorite crime-fighting pigeon. How is your **REAL PIGEONS** squad going, Tumbler?"

"This is Megabat," giggles Tumbler.
"My best bat friend."

Suddenly, Rock isn't scared. He's amazed.

"I thought you bats might be like crows. But you're **AWESOME**, Megabat!"

"I guess I am a tad awesome,"
says Megabat.
"Hey, do you want to hear a song?
I can sing in sonar, you know."

"Actually," says Tumbler, "LET'S GO FLYING!"

"GREAT IDEA!" says Megabat.

"ZOOM ZOOM ZOOMITY ZOOM!"

"Let's follow the bats,"
Tumbler whispers to Rock.

"And look out for traps. Don't tell Megabat,
though. I don't want to ruin his night!"

Rock leaps out of his pot. "Bats are my new
favorite creatures!"

"Sure, fly off. The rest
of us will keep an eye
on the street."

Rock and Tumbler glide through the sky with the bats.

"Is that a flying cactus?"

It is very exciting.

"Got any new **Flight Moves?**" Megabat asks.

"**Sure do! I call this the MAGIC CARPET,**" says Tumbler.

"Bravo!" cries Megabat.

But even as she bends and twirls through the air, Tumbler keeps a close watch for any traps.

"So what do bats do at night?" asks Rock.

"Lots of things," says Megabat. "We ride the power lines."

"NO TRAPS HERE!"

"We hang out with owls and finish their words."

"Hoot-" "-er!"

"Hoot-" "-enanny!"

"Hoo-"

"Let the Dogs Out?"

"NO TRAPS HERE EITHER!"

"And we ride dogs around."

"Giddyup!"

"NO TRAPS!"

Rock is having a ball.

But this whole time, Tumbler has been looking for traps. "Aren't you worried we might get trapped?" she says.

"Worrying is not fun," Rock cries. "Having fun is fun!"

"Yes," says Tumbler nervously. "But I think we're getting off track."

The bats land in a fruit tree.

"I thought you **LIKED** flying with bats?" says Rock.

"We're supposed to be watching for traps," says Tumbler. "And the **BAT TRAPPER!** Remember?"

"Oh, I know who the **BAT TRAPPER** is," says Megabat.

"What?" cry Rock and Tumbler. "Who?"

"There's a famous wildlife photographer in town," says Megabat.

ROBERTA MAPLESYRUP IN TOWN

Famous bat photographer to photograph local bats...

"You think she's the
BAT TRAPPER?" says Tumbler.

Megabat nods. "She probably wants to trap us so that she can take better photos of us being beautiful."

"That makes sense," says Rock. "Bats are pretty beautiful!"

"Are you thinking what I'm thinking?" says Tumbler.

Rock nods.

"Being a bat is TOTALLY COO!"

"No," says Tumbler.

"We need to find the photographer!"

They don't see any traps that night. But Tumbler isn't taking any chances. The next day, she flies off again.

"I'm going to look for that photographer," she says. "Do you want to come?"

"No, I have something else to do," says Rock.

When she is gone, Rock goes on a hunt.

And finds some odds and ends.

stretchy old tights

twigs

berry

Rock has decided he doesn't want
to be a cactus anymore.

Or a pigeon.

He wants to be a . . .

. . . BAT!

CHAPTER 3

Rock shows everyone his new costume.
It doesn't go well.

"Are you dressed as bait?
For the **BAT TRAPPER?**"

"Are you dressed
for Halloween?"

"It's a vampire!"

Rock is confused.

Being a bat is **TOTALLY COO!** So why
doesn't anyone like his costume?

He sits down unhappily.

Just as he does, someone stops to look at him.

It is Roberta Maplesyrup, the photographer.

"I've never seen a wild bat on a step before," she says.

"Is she the BAT TRAPPER?"

But she doesn't trap him.

She **photographs** him.

Finally—someone likes his costume!

ROCK DANCES FOR JOY.

"You're so cute," says the photographer.
"I wish I could take you home with me."

Rock stops dancing. That's the kind of thing
a **BAT TRAPPER** would say.

He flies up to the window ledge. Just in case.

When Tumbler returns, the sun is setting.
Rock tells her what happened.

"We need to warn the bats,"

says Tumbler,

**"in case Roberta Maplesyrup
is the trapper."**

"Nice costume,"
she adds.
"You really are batty!"

The pigeons wait patiently for
the bats to show up.

They wait long into the night.

But the bats never come.

The **BAT TRAPPER**
must have struck once more!

Rock and Tumbler go looking for the bats.
They are very worried.

They search all night.

But the bats are nowhere to be found. Have
they been batnapped for good this time?

The sun starts to rise.

"We've looked in **EVERY SINGLE TREE,**" sighs Tumbler.

"We need to have an **EMERGENCY SQUAD MEETING,**" says Rock.

They fly into the garbage. Again.

"Is that another creepy bat?"

Inside the garbage can, all the pigeons look at Rock.

"Isn't it a little dangerous to be a bat right now?" says Frillbuck.

"Are you trying to be bait?" says Grandpouter.

"No," says Rock. "Why does everyone keep saying that? I just like dressing up. And bats are awesome."

"We don't have time for this," says Tumbler.

She explains that the bats are missing again.

"We need a plan," says Grandpouter.

"Maybe we should set a **TRAP** for the **BAT TRAPPER!**" says Frillback. "I know who we could use for bait."

Rock is wondering if maybe he shouldn't have dressed like a bat, when suddenly . . .

EVERYTHING GOES DARK.

The pigeons are
TOSSED
around.

What is
happening?

Someone is taking out the trash.

"Get out of my can, bat!"

The garbage collector throws the bag toward the truck.

The pigeons poke their heads out.

"AHHHHHHH!"

THEY ARE ABOUT TO BE CRUSHED!

Frillback bursts out of the bag.

And saves them **JUST** in time.

"I really **HATE** garbage meetings," says Frillback.

RUMBLE RUMBLE

"**Thank you for saving us!**"

cries Tumbler.
"**You're a coo friend, Frillback!**"

Rock glares out at the bat-hating garbage collector.

Is *he* the
BAT TRAPPER?

Back on the street, the pigeons borrow a bird-cage from the garden store. And set a trap.

"Don't worry," says Tumbler. "If the **BAT TRAPPER** turns up, we'll spring into action."

"OK," says Rock.

It's not very fun being bait.

The other pigeons hide and watch.

After a while, the garbage collector appears.

So does the photographer.

One of them must be the **BAT TRAPPER.**

But which one is it?

CHAPTER 4

Suddenly, there is a flash of darkness.

"Uh-oh."

CLICK!

"HELP!"

The **BAT TRAPPER** has struck.

"Let's go!" cries Tumbler.

Meanwhile, Rock opens a secret door.

"YEAH, SECRET DOOR!"

And flies out the bottom of the cage.

"Hello, BAT TRAPPER!"
says Rock.
"Or should I say—
MEGABAT?"

Megabat is surprised
to see Rock.

118

So surprised that he doesn't notice the other **REAL PIGEONS**. Or the garbage bag.

"GOTCHA!"

cries Rock.

The pigeons take Megabat
back to the can.

"I can't believe
YOU'RE the
BAT
TRAPPER!"
cries Tumbler.

Megabat hangs his head in shame. "I just wanted to be famous," he says. "And to be the **only** bat in Roberta Maplesyrup's photos. I'm such a show-off."

Tumbler is mad.

"I ought to sock you one," she says.

"Don't do it! Your feathers will just feel nice on his face!" Rock yells.

"Where have you trapped the other bats this time?" says Grandpouter.

"In the garden store," sighs Megabat.

"I led them all there last night. I covered the tree with

SUPER-GLUE!"

"HELP!"

"But then I couldn't find Roberta Maplesyrup anyway," says Megabat sadly. "I'll never be famous."

Two teenagers walk past. They are talking loudly. And looking at their phones.

"Have you seen the dancing bat? It's going viral."

"Is that ... Rock?" Homey asks.

Megabat is **FURIOUS.** "That should have been me!" he screams. "You stole my fame, Rock!"

He bursts free of the garbage bag and flies away.

"You haven't seen the last of me, **REAL PIGEONS!**"

"Oh dear."

The **REAL PIGEONS** quickly fly to the garden store and rescue all the bats.

"Bats, you are FREE!"

"Bats, you are FREE!"

"Bats, you are FREE!"

Rock explains that Megabat was the **BAT TRAPPER.**

"Of course! He was in the perfect position to lay all the traps!"

"He always was a big show-off!"

"Thanks for catching him!"

Megabat got away.

But he won't batnap the other bats anymore.

Frillback pulls off the last bat.

"You should fly with us sometime, Frillback," say the bats. "Your feathers would look beautiful in the moonlight!"

"You bats aren't so bad!" Frillback blushes.

"Thanks for setting us FREEEE!"

Rock takes off his bat costume.

"I've had enough of being a bat," he says.
"I only want to be a **REAL PIGEON** now!"

"REAL PIGEONS
are totally coo!"

"I know Megabat was bad,"
says Tumbler. "But he was
my best bat friend."

"You've got other friends,"
says Rock.

"REAL PIGEONS
make **REAL FRIENDS!"**

"And we can still do batty things," says Rock.

"Really?" says Tumbler.

"Absolutely." Rock grins. "All of us!"

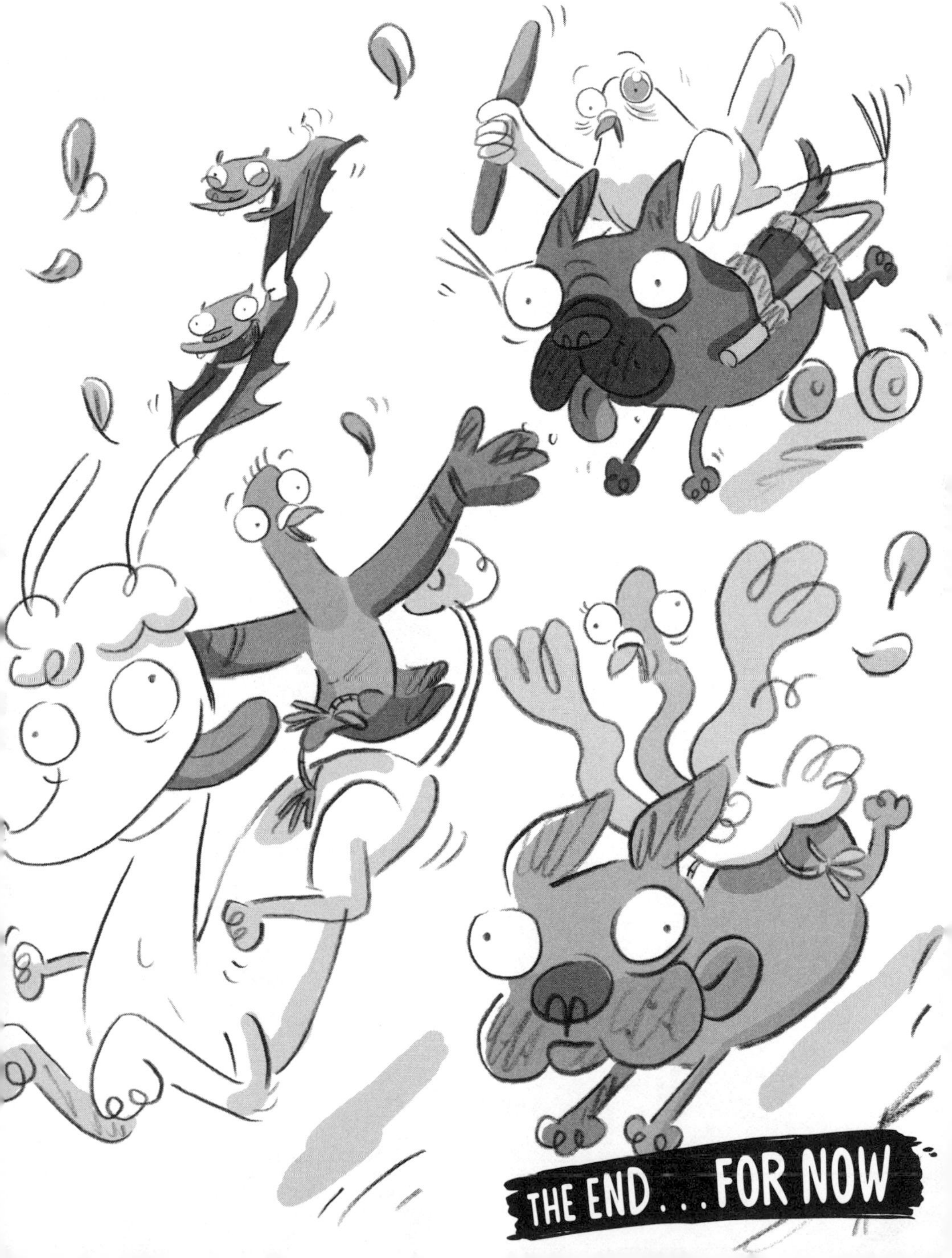
THE END . . . FOR NOW

ALTHOUGH...

THERE IS ONE MORE THING.

In the middle of a park

on the other side of the city,

a bird is trying to get his dinner.

"Who would put a worm in the bottom of a bottle?"

"AHHH!"

A dark figure flies down from above.

Jungle Crow looks up in surprise.

"Heard you've had some pigeon troubles," says Megabat. "Me too. Interested in teaming up? We could make a great duo."

"Why, yes!"

TO BE CONTINUED . . . .

Do you want floor fries with that?
sticky!
PART THREE
DANGER
AT THE FOOD TRUCK FAIR
yum! yum! sausages!

CHAPTER 1

Rock and the **REAL PIGEONS** march forward.
They have an important new mission.

"I hope you know where you're going, Frillback," says Rock.

"Trust me," says Frillback. "This is the place."

"We're here!"

The pigeons have arrived at a . . .

FOOD TRUCK FAIR

FOOD TRUCKS MAKE THE
AIR SMELL **DELICIOUS!**

THE TRUCKS STOP HERE

Now the pigeons must solve
their greatest mystery yet.

WHAT TO EAT FOR DINNER?

137

Rock is excited.

He is usually busy being a **MASTER OF DISGUISE.** And fighting crime. And protecting animals.

But tonight, dinner is the only mission.

"REAL PIGEONS SOLVE DINNER!"

BREAD CRUMBS?

BREAD CRUMBS?

MORE BREAD CRUMBS?

EVEN MORE BREAD CRUMBS?

"I want to visit the food truck that sells sausages," says Frillback eagerly. "Sausages are my favorite food."

"Dude!" says Homey.
"What about bread crumbs?"

Frillback shrugs. "I think sausages are way more **coo**."

"**Whaaaaat?**"

Rock thinks sausages are silly.

They look like bananas that got burned in a fire.

Suddenly, Rock hears something strange.
A boy is walking past.

tick tick
stink

MARIA'S
SAUSAGES

Did you know pigeons have **super ears?**

While humans are experts at TALKING . . .

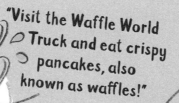

"Visit the Waffle World Truck and eat crispy pancakes, also known as waffles!"

"Visit the Sandwich Truck and eat the best sandwiches since sliced bread!"

"Visit the Banana Truck and eat tiny versions of me!"

. . . pigeons are experts at LISTENING.

"Can you guys hear that?"

tick
tick
stink

The ticking doesn't sound like a clock.
And it's too loud to be a watch.
Suddenly, Rock knows exactly what it is.

tick
tick
stink

"I think there is a STINK BOMB in that boy's bag!" he says.

But the boy is gone.

The **REAL PIGEONS** have an **EMERGENCY SQUAD MEETING.**

Their mission is no longer to have dinner.

It is to stop the bomb. Before it causes a big stink—and turns all the food bad!

"Who is that boy?" asks Rock. "And why does he want to ruin everyone's dinner?"

"I don't know, but we have to find him—fast!" says Grandpouter.

CHAPTER 2

The boy is now somewhere in the crowd of humans. So Homey volunteers to find him.

"Homing pigeons can find anything!"

But crowds don't mix well with pigeons. And that includes Homey.

"SHOO!"

"SHOO!"

"Finding this kid might be harder than I first imagined."

Grandpouter has another idea.

"Rock, can you dress up as a human?" he asks.
"To move through the crowd and look for the boy?"

Rock looks down at his little pigeon toes unhappily.
"No," he says. "Human disguises are too hard."

"BLAH! BLAH! BLAH!"

big

good at talking

skin

HUMAN
VS.
PIGEON

little

better at listening

feathers

Rock has tried to dress up as *parts* of humans before.

But he has always failed.

Either he is **too feathery** . . .

"I'm a knee!"

or his **costume** is no good . . .

"I'm an arm."

"I'm a hand."

or his **tail shows.**

"I'm sorry, Grandpouter," says Rock. "But I can't."

"OK," says Grandpouter. "We'll think of something else." But he sounds disappointed.

Rock feels terrible.

What's the point of being a **MASTER OF DISGUISE** if you can't dress up as a human?

"They're just so **BIG!**"

The pigeons decide to split up
to look for the boy.

"REAL PIGEONS STOP STINK BOMBS!"

Grandpouter, Homey, and Tumbler fly off,
leaving Rock and Frillback behind.

"I would prefer to
dress up like a human."

"I would prefer to
eat a sausage."

Rock tries to concentrate. Maybe the boy is hiding under a food truck?

"Can you lift that truck up with your super strength?" he says. "And I'll look under it."

"No," says Frillback. "I'm not doing anything until I eat a sausage."

"What?" asks Rock. He is confused.

Since when does Frillback care about food more than a **REAL PIGEONS** mission?

At that moment, Rock sees a girl drop a sausage.

He is off in a flash.

"Here's your sausage. Now let's get back to the search."

Except it's not a sausage.

"That's a hot dog," says Frillback. "Hot dogs look like blushing bananas. I want a SAUSAGE!"

Suddenly, the pigeons hear a familiar sound.
They can't believe it.

tick tick stink

"That's him!"
cries Rock.

They rush after the boy,

who disappears . . .

. . . into a tent.

MADAME VELLA:
FORTUNE-TELLER
NO TICKET, NO ENTRY

"No humans—
or birds—get in
without a ticket!"

The pigeons can go no farther.

Rock and Frillback need to get inside that tent somehow.

Rock wishes he could dress up like a human and buy tickets.

He searches the area in case someone has dropped a ticket. But he finds only random bits and pieces.

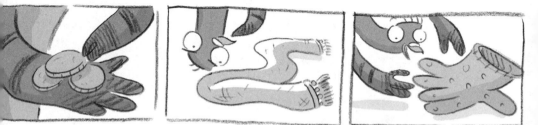

Which give him an idea.

He puts the glove on.

wiggle wiggle

Wraps the scarf around his tail.

dizzy!

And flies up to the ticket booth.

Rock can't be a whole human. But he can be **PART** of a human.

"Two tickets?" asks the lady. "Here you go, kid."

SUCCESS!

The pigeons go into the tent.

"Welcome," says a shadow.

"Did you see a boy come in here?" asks Rock nervously. "With a ticking bag?"

"Come closer," says the shadow. "I will tell all."

The pigeons fly up to the table.

It's a birdcage.

· MR. KEET ·

Mr. Keet must be Madame Vella's pet.

But the cage is pretty small. The parakeet looks cramped.

"Hello," says Rock. "Do you want me to set you free?"

"All in good time," squawks Mr. Keet. "Why don't I tell your fortune first? Before Madame Vella returns from the bathroom."

· MR. KEET ·

Mr. Keet picks up a card and writes a note on it.

He tosses it to the pigeons.

You'll find the two you seek, if out the back you take a peek.

Rock is confused. "We're not looking for **TWO** people," he says. "We're looking for **ONE** boy."

"I know," says the parakeet mysteriously. "But that boy is on his own journey. So you should really take my advice."

EXIT

Rock thanks Mr. Keet.
Then he opens the cage.

"Now be free!"

"BYEEEE!"

MR. KEET

Rock and Frillback run
to the back of the tent.

They peek outside.

And they can't
believe what they see.

CHAPTER 3

IT'S JUNGLE CROW.

AND MEGABAT!

"I'm so glad we met!"

"You're my baddie from another daddy!"

What are they doing together?

Rock is horrified. But he and Frillback need to get closer to hear what Jungle Crow and Megabat are saying.

They can't fly. Because it will make a **FLAPPY** noise.

They can't walk. Because it will make a **SCRATCHY** noise.

They will have to tiptoe. On their feathers.

The pigeons come to a stop just behind the two villains.

"Putting the stinker in that bag was easy!"

"The plan is going perfectly."

So the stink bomb belongs to Jungle Crow and Megabat!

The boy has no idea he is carrying it around. It could ruin everyone's dinner at any moment.

Rock isn't scared anymore. He's **MAD.** He flies up.

"Why are you doing this?" he cries. "People come to the **FOOD TRUCK FAIR** to eat dinner without a big stink! And so do pigeons!"

"AHHHHHH!"

Jungle Crow and Megabat are shocked. They weren't expecting Rock Pigeon. And they take off.

"Come back here!"

yell Rock and Frillback.

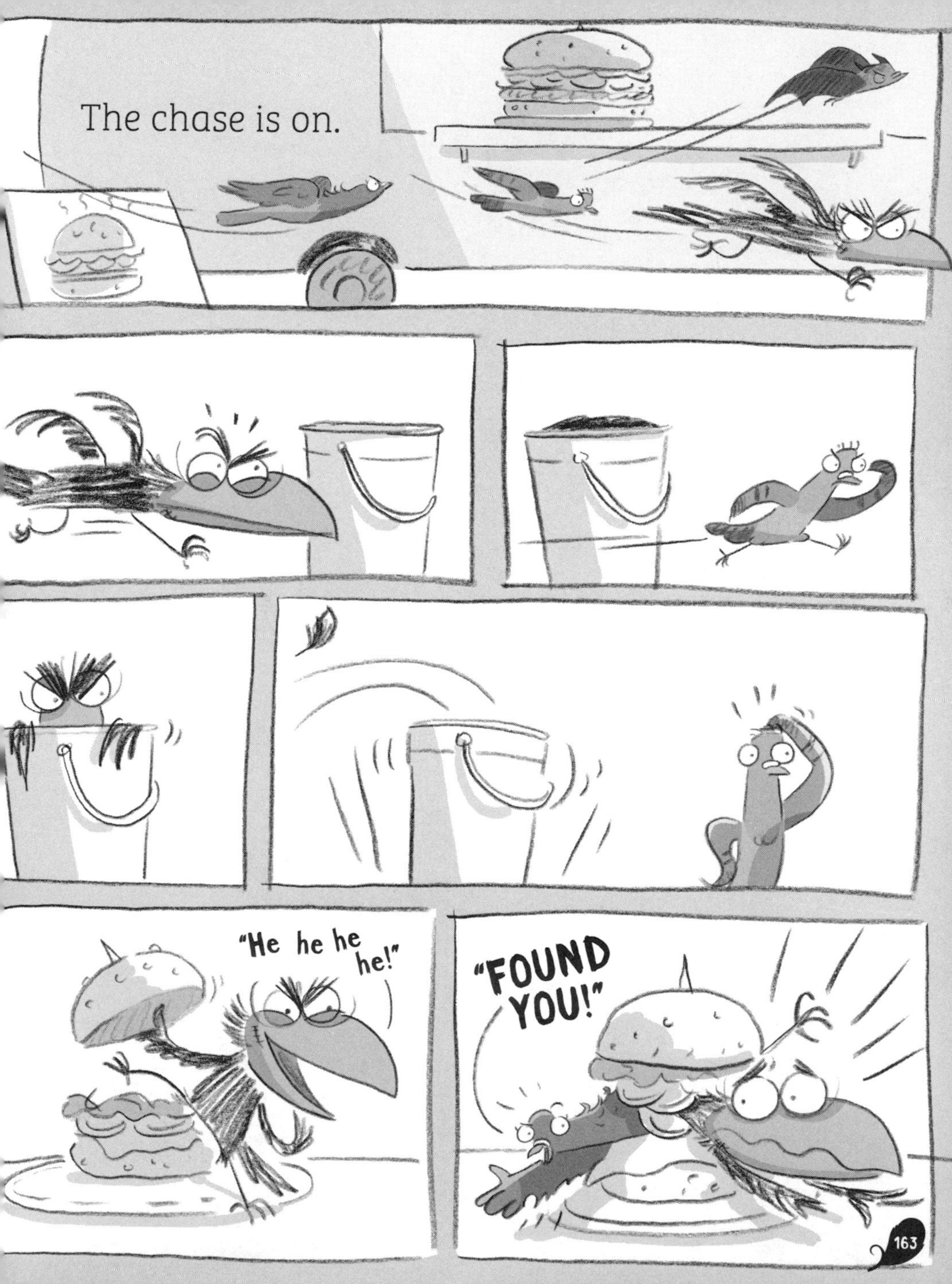
The chase is on.
"He he he he!"
"FOUND YOU!"

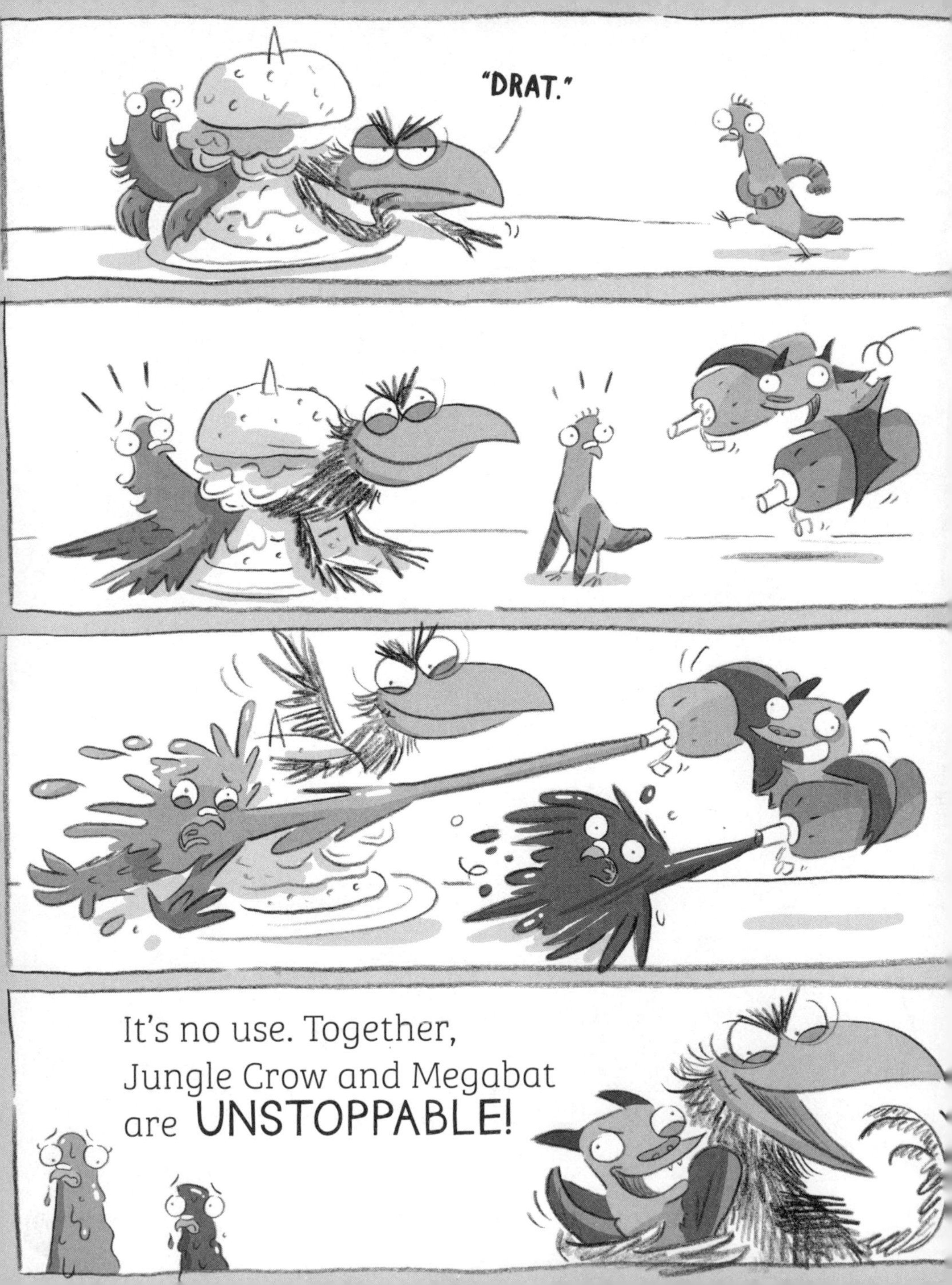
"DRAT."
It's no use. Together,
Jungle Crow and Megabat
are UNSTOPPABLE!

The REAL PIGEONS
meet back at the pizza box.

"What are Jungle Crow and Megabat thinking?" says Tumbler.

"I still haven't eaten a single sausage," says Frillback.

"We can't find the boy," says Rock. "But he's here somewhere."

"Then we need to get the humans away from the Food Truck Fair!" says Grandpouter. "Before the stink bomb explodes. Humans are very sensitive to **BAD SMELLS.**"

Rock wants to stop Jungle Crow and Megabat himself.

But Grandpouter turns to Frillback.

"Frillback, use your **PIGEON POWER** to throw things around—chairs, garbage cans, dogs,"

says Grandpouter.

"That should **SCARE** everyone away."

"I can't,"

says Frillback.

That's when Rock realizes something is seriously wrong with her.

"Have you lost your **PIGEON POWER?**"

he asks.

"I get my super strength from sausages,"

says Frillback.

"But I haven't eaten one in a week. A nice lady called Maria gives me sausages from her food truck."

So that's why Frillback wanted a sausage so badly!

"See! I can't even pick you up!"

Luckily, Rock has a different idea.

Maybe he can't dress up and pretend to be human.

FOOD TRUCK FAIR

THE TRUCKS STOP HERE

But there's already a **PRETEND HUMAN** here!

Rock makes each pigeon hide in a different part of the Food Truck Fair's scarecrow.

Homey in the left leg.

Tumbler in the right leg.

Frillback takes an arm.

Grandpouter takes the other arm.

And Rock decides to be the human face.

He pulls off the buttons and carrot.

The pigeons are going to scare all the humans away . . .

by bringing a scarecrow to life.

The pigeons stick out their wings and flap hard.

Together, they are strong enough to move straw. And make the scarecrow walk.

Rock is finally wearing a human disguise.

Kind of.

Now they must scare the humans away.

Homey and Tumbler wiggle
the scarecrow's legs.

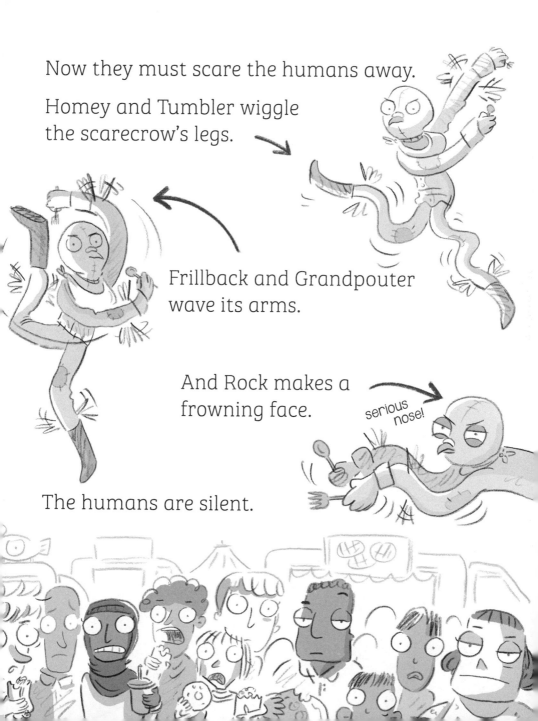

Frillback and Grandpouter
wave its arms.

And Rock makes a
frowning face.

serious
nose!

The humans are silent.

Until they burst into applause and cheers.

"It must be a robot scarecrow!"

"Very believable!"

The plan is a disaster. The humans aren't scared. They're amused!

But then Rock sees a familiar face. It's Mr. Keet.

"Have we met before? I never forget a face."

Rock sticks his neck out. "Hello again!"

"Oh, it's you!" says Mr. Keet. "I just saw the boy you were looking for. He was heading for that giant sausage."

Then the parakeet sees Madame Vella, the fortune-teller, walking around with her empty cage.

"I'd better get going."

Mr. Keet says quickly.

"Byeeeeee!"

"Let's fly to that giant sausage, **REAL PIGEONS!**" gasps Rock.

The pigeons flap harder than ever. The scarecrow lifts off the ground and flies through the air. It leaves the crowd behind.

"The robot scarecrow can fly!"

"This is what the future looks like!"

The giant sausage is on top of a food truck. Suddenly, the boy reappears.

"Hi, Mom! I've been looking all over for you. I didn't know where you parked the food truck!"

Oh no!
Maria is the boy's mother.

Rock is about to dive for the boy's bag when more bad news arrives.

"REAL PIGEONS!" shouts Jungle Crow. "You destroyed my **MONSTER CROW!**"

"And my claim to fame," adds Megabat.

"Now we'll destroy you!"

Jungle Crow and Megabat tear the scarecrow apart.

Rock's human disguise has failed. Again.

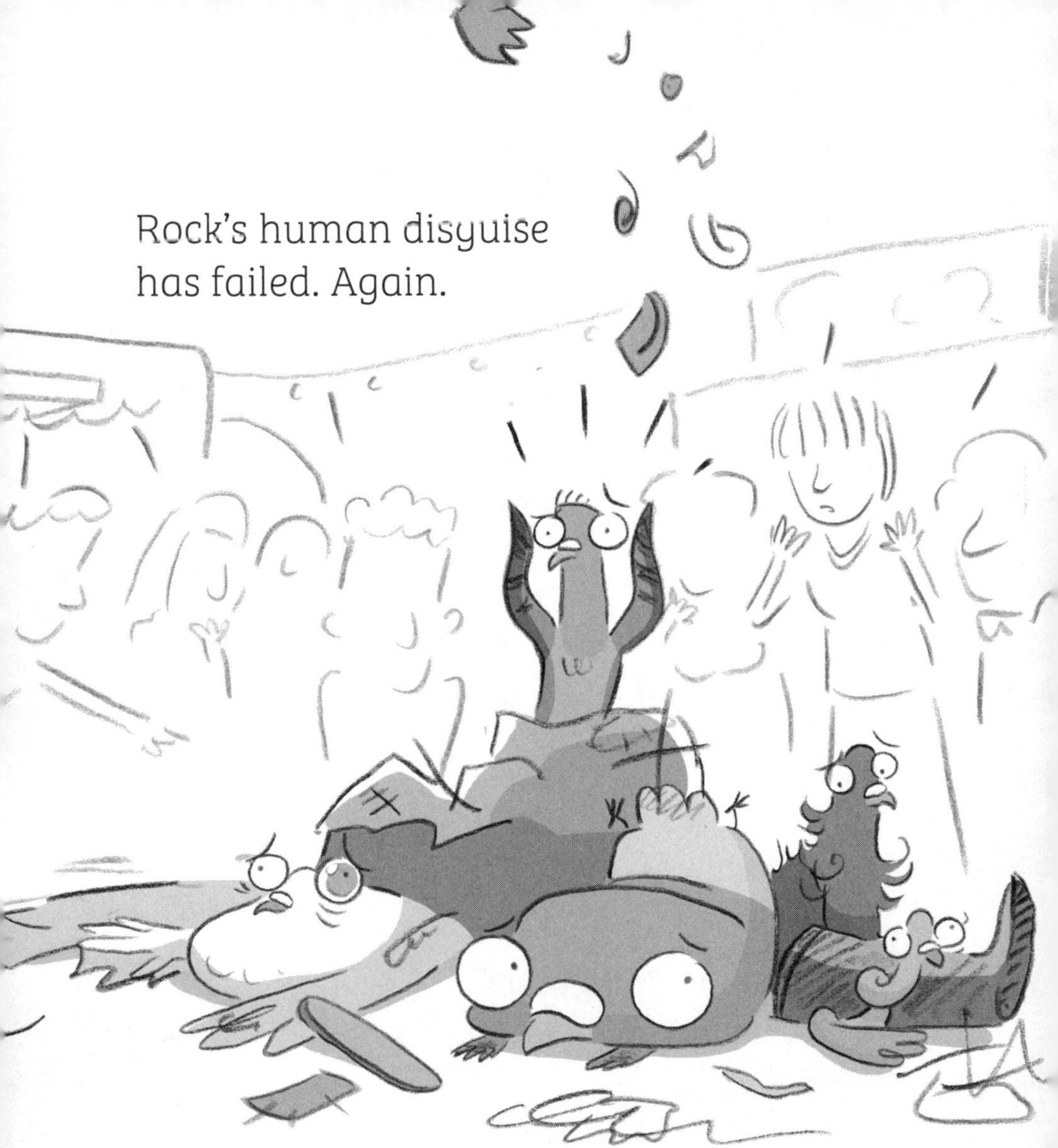

He is not a **MASTER OF DISGUISE.**

He is a **DISASTER OF DISGUISE.**

CHAPTER 4

The stink bomb is still in the boy's bag.

And lots of humans have gathered around.

All thanks to Jungle Crow and Megabat.

"Is now a bad time to quickly eat a sausage?" asks Frillback.

"YES!" says everybody.

But Rock understands.

Frillback just wants her powers back.

Grandpouter pokes his stick at Jungle Crow and Megabat. "Why do you want to set off a stink bomb at the fair?"

"To drive all the humans away," says Jungle Crow. "So I can make this a **CROWS-ONLY FOOD FAIR!**"

"And so I can get famous," says Megabat.

"We found this handsome creature at the site of the explosion."

"We found the bag on the ground," Jungle Crow adds. "So we put the stink bomb in it and hung it from a tree—for **MAXIMUM** badness."

"But humans **MAKE** all the food at the Food Truck Fair," cries Rock. "If there are no humans, there won't be any more food!"

Jungle Crow looks shocked.

"Whaaat?" he says. "I didn't think of that!"

"And that's not all," says Rock. "The bag is **HERE.** Which means you won't just get rid of the humans. You'll spoil all the food you want to eat too!"

"What do you mean, the bag is *here*?" says Megabat with a shudder. Rock points.

The boy is holding the bag out to Maria.

"Mom, I found one of your bags in a tree," he says.

tick   tick

stink

MARIA'S SAUSAGES

MARIA'S SAUSAGES

"It will go off any moment!" cries Jungle Crow. "If we can't save the food, then we have to save the humans!"

"**YES,**" agrees Rock. "But how?"

Rock looks around in panic.

"Leave this to the **REAL PIGEONS,**" he says.

He has a plan. And he only needs two things for it.

A brand-new disguise.

And a sausage.

"Frillback, can you please eat a sausage?" Rock asks.

"I thought you'd never ask," says Frillback.

Maria throws a sausage to Frillback, who gobbles it down greedily.

"There's that pigeon who loves my sausages."

Frillback's strength returns immediately.

"You're back!"
cries Rock happily.

"Now I need your muscles."

The pigeons dart behind a bush.

They pluck all the feathers from Rock's bottom.

Wrap the scarecrow shirt around Rock and Frillback.

And draw a face.

Rock has finally made a human disguise.

"You make a pretty coo baby, Rock!"

"GOO GOO GA GA!"

The crowd thinks it's a real baby. Rock and Frillback fly over their heads. And the humans freak out.

Just as Rock had hoped.

"OMG, how is that baby floating?"

"It doesn't matter— just save it!"

The crowd chases them.

The pigeons fly out of the **FOOD TRUCK FAIR.**

Down the street.

And into a park.

The pigeons land.

They are a long way from the stink bomb now.

The humans grab the floating baby.
And are disappointed to learn the truth.

"Aw, it's just a shirt with some pigeons inside."

But the pigeons have saved everyone
from the **TERRIBLE SMELL.**

Back at the **FOOD TRUCK FAIR,** there is a fight over the bag.

"These creatures are crazy," says the boy. "Why do they want this bag?"

"Maybe there's something in it?" says Maria.

The bag finally rips open. And the stink bomb falls to the ground.

IT'S ABOUT TO EXPLODE.

They are going to get **STINKED!**

Frillback swoops
down from the sky.

"Time to get rid
of this thing,"
she says.

Using all her
PIGEON POWER,

FRILLBACK **FLINGS**
THE STINK BOMB
HIGH INTO THE SKY.

10:0

It flies like a rocket.

And goes . . .

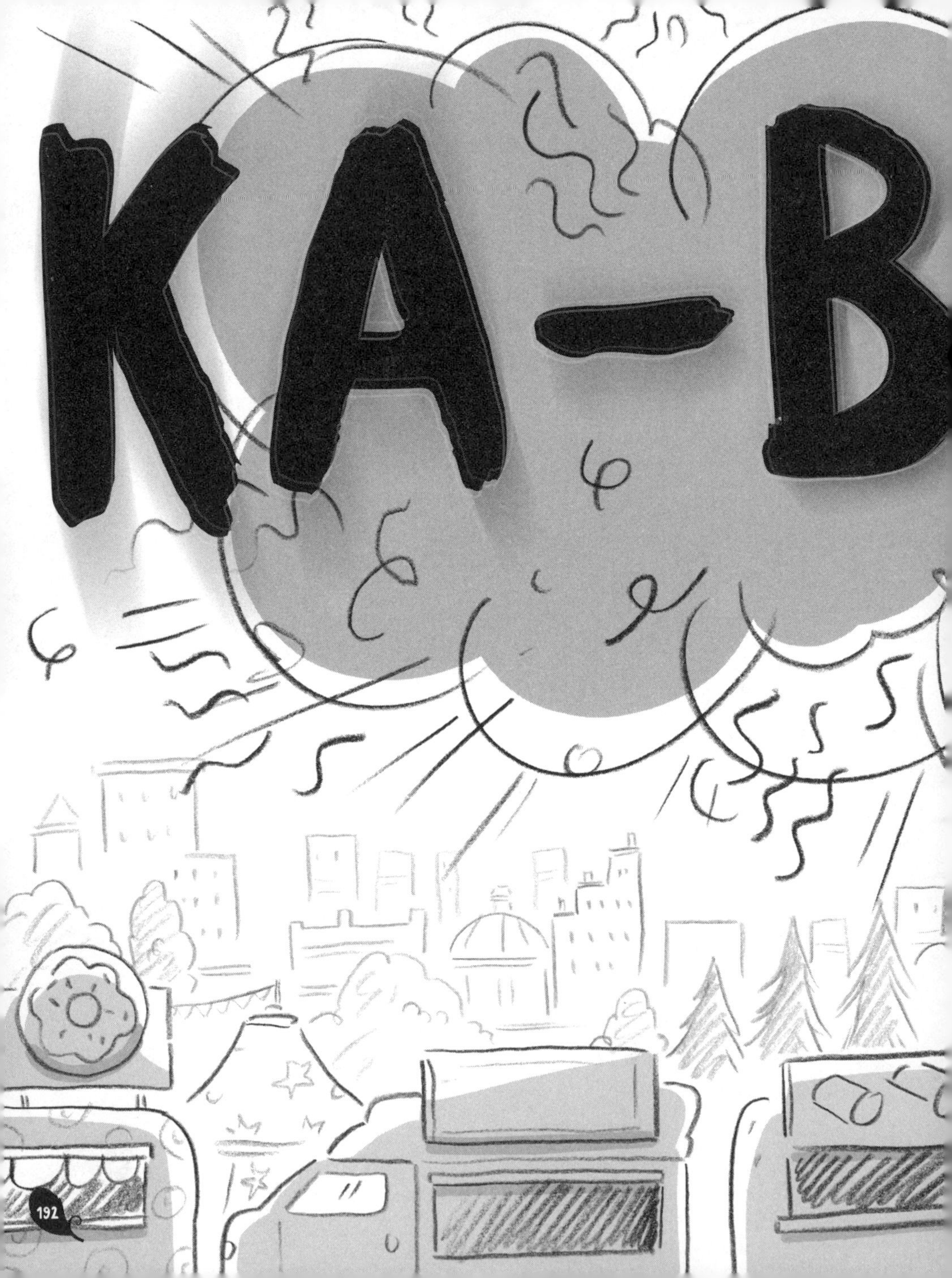
KA-B

OOM!

"You did it!"
cheers Rock.
"The food AND the
humans are saved!"

Sadly, Megabat and Jungle Crow go straight back to their old ways.

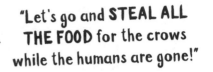

"Let's go and **STEAL ALL THE FOOD** for the crows while the humans are gone!"

"That was a big explosion. The **TV** crews are probably on their way."

Rock is wondering what to do with them . . . when two hands reach down.

And shove them into a cage.

Madame Vella, the fortune teller, is very pleased.

"I've been looking for some more winged friends," she says. "You two will do nicely."

"Grrrr."

"At least I'm finally in show business."

Jungle Crow and Megabat are locked up at last.

The humans are all safe.

The stink bomb is gone.

There is only one thing left to do.

"EAT DINNER!"

"Do you pigeons want some sausages?" asks Maria. *"There's no one else to eat them."*

The **REAL PIGEONS** have a sausage feast.

"I have to admit, **PIGS**—sausages are pretty tasty," says Homey.

"Because they're made out of meat and . . . **BREAD CRUMBS**," cries Frillback.

"DINNER IS SERVED ... AND SOLVED!"

Rock is happy.
He has mastered a
human disguise.

And he smiles—
in two places.

wiggle
wiggle

THE END

UNFORTUNATELY . . .

While the REAL PIGEONS enjoy their sausages, **TROUBLE** LURKS NEARBY.

A shadowy figure moves through the FOOD TRUCK FAIR.

Stealing all the butter in sight.

Carrying it away into the night.

And whispering creepily,

"This butter is going
to make a lot of birds
VERY UNHAPPY!"

HOW CAN BUTTER MAKE BIRDS UNHAPPY?

WHO IS THIS MYSTERIOUS BUTTER THIEF?

AND WILL ROCK'S BOTTOM FEATHERS GROW
BACK IN TIME FOR THE NEXT STORY?

FIND
OUT
IN

REAL PIGEONS
2
EAT DANGER

ANDREW McDONALD   BEN WOOD

MEET THE
TEAM

ANDREW McDONALD

is a writer from Melbourne, Australia. He lives with a lovely lady and a bouncy son and enjoys baking his own bread (which he eats down to the last bread crumb—sorry, pigeons!). Visit Andrew at mrandrewmcdonald.com.

BEN WOOD

has illustrated more than twenty-five books for children. When Ben isn't drawing, he likes to eat food! His favorite foods include overstuffed burritos, green spaghetti, and big bags of chips! Yum! Visit Ben at benwood.com.au.

BEN WOOD
awesome
illustrator

ANDREW McDONALD
clever
author

DID YOU KNOW REAL PIGEONS ARE REAL-LIFE PIGEONS?

FRILLBACK PIGEON

Known as a "fancy pigeon." Humans have bred them to be covered in curly feathers. These birds don't need to use hair curlers!

ROCK PIGEON

The most common pigeon in the world. Gray with two black stripes on each wing. Very good at blending in!

TUMBLER PIGEON

Known to tumble or somersault while in flight. They fly normally before unexpectedly doing aerial acrobatics.

HOMING PIGEON

Has the incredible ability to fly long distances and return home from very far away. They were used to deliver letters many years ago.

POUTER PIGEON

The big bubble that looks like a chest is actually called a crop. Pouters store food in their crops before releasing it to their stomachs. Yuck!

FIND OUT MORE AT
WWW.REALPIGEONS.COM!